Ten Short Mysteries

Ten Short Mysteries

Robert G. Davis

iUniverse, Inc.
Bloomington

Ten Short Mysteries

iUniverse books may be ordered through booksellers or by contacting:

iUniverse
1663 Liberty Drive
Bloomington, IN 47403
www.iuniverse.com
1-800-Authors (1-800-288-4677)

ISBN: 978-1-4759-4868-4 (sc)
ISBN: 978-1-4759-4870-7 (hc)
ISBN: 978-1-4759-4869-1 (ebk)

Library of Congress Control Number: 2012916889

Printed in the United States of America

iUniverse rev. date: 09/25/2012

CONTENTS

GREMLINS

On a slow cool August afternoon deep in the northern forest, they sat by the slow rambling brook. There was no object in getting into anything more complex then turning the cards on the table. After all, it was almost time to walk the trap lines and gather up any new catch.

It was Earl's night to check the river lines and Joe's to check the mountain and creek lines. As they finished their afternoon tea and prepared to depart for their lines, they heard a rather unusual noise coming from the east forest.

Looking at each other, they decided they had better check it out quickly as they each had several hours of walking ahead of them on the trap lines.

As they cautiously moved into the eastern meadow towards the forest, they were careful not to converse and make any noise as they wanted to see what was there.

As they carefully moved into the forest, they were very slow and deliberate in stalking the noise that was seemingly just ahead. After moving into the forest several hundred feet, they looked at each other as Earl questions, "is it moving ahead of us or what"?

As they turned to return to the cabin so they could begin their line checks, they heard a faint groan as if something was hurt and needing help. Stopping in their tracks they listened intently, trying to get a fix on the sound.

Nothing.

They looked for any signs that may have been left by whatever.

Still nothing.

Now they were really wondering if it would be safe to spend several hours away from their cabin and not know what they might be coming back to.

Faced with such a decision, they returned to the cabin and started to discuss their choices. Would one go and check the more important river trail and the other stay behind to watch the cabin and observe the meadow for whatever may be out there. After all, it would be close to dark by the time either line was checked and they returned to the cabin.

Listening carefully for any sounds, they had not heard anything for a few minutes. Now they were about thirty minutes late leaving the cabin and that would make checking and returning time very late, maybe even after dark.

That itself would be dangerous. But how to decide on who would stay, who would go. Jokingly, Joe suggested, "We could flip a coin." That would also take time as they were not in the habit of keeping coins out when at the cabin for several weeks at a time.

Earl spoke softly, "We had better cover our own trails tonight, it is late already." That would mean leaving the cabin for several hours, but it must be done.

As they started out in their respective directions, they looked back at each other wondering if they were doing the right thing. Well, only time will tell, they thought.

The sun was long into the mountain valley when Joe reached the end of the line where he could start back and check each trap. He knew that he would have to hurry along the trails as it would be dark in some of the lower valleys he had to travel.

Stopping at each trap would also take several minutes as he would have to remove the catch and reset the trap. He thought about jogging from trap to trap until he had enough catch to slow him down. Most of the trail home was downhill from where he was starting the check.

As he reached his first trap, he noticed something wrong. The area around the trap was disturbed. He stopped and looked around.

He did not like the looks of what he was seeing. Had something taken the bait and got caught in the trap. Maybe something had taken the catch and made the mess when trying to get the creature out of the trap.

He looked around for other signs of disturbances. There were several small trees that had been broken and leaves stripped. As he moved toward the trap, he noticed that the trap was in place and still set.

He felt relieved to know that the trap was still secure. But what made the big disturbance. He did not need to take the time to investigate this tonight. He was already late and had more to think about.

As long as the trap was secure, he must return to the trail and keep moving down the valley. The trail was rather steep and narrow in several places and he needed to get through those areas before the sun was completely behind the mountain.

It would be dark within a half hour once the sun had fully set. Jogging down the trail he was cautious to look for any other signs that might arouse his interest.

It did not take long to arrive at the big bend in the first narrow, steep downhill grade. Slowing to a walk, he thought he heard noises coming from his west side.

Thinking he did not have time to check it out he navigated the narrow downward trail for several hundred feet. As he prepared to step off the trail to check his second trap, he was confronted by a rather large herd of deer that had been spooked.

This was really getting to Joe. First his trap area is messed up, now he comes face to face with a herd of spooked deer.

Earl, in the meantime, was having a great time checking his traps along the river. He was observing a new nest of birds probably the last of the year and several rabbits.

He reached his turn around point in what appeared to be near record time. What had made him move so swiftly to this point? But from here back to the cabin, it was all up hill. He observed several beavers along the river trail and several muskrats playing on a log in the river.

Thinking they would not be home for supper tonight, Earl called to them, "You boys better get home soon." He kept moving toward his first trap.

As Earl started to move toward his first trap, he noticed a pair of beavers playing again on the bank of the swift moving river.

He knew he would not have time to watch them for long as he still had an hour of checking and walking to return to the cabin. Arriving at his first trap, he noticed it was empty and fully set. Well, keep moving and save time.

From this point he had to go into several backwater areas. That would mean balancing on several logs to cross some swamp waters. He needed to get past them before it got to dark.

There were also several traps set in the area that would be hard to reach if the water was a little high. As he started to follow the trail into the first of the backwaters, he noticed his second trap was sprung.

This would raise the anxiety level of any trapper. He approached the trap as he usually would, slowly. Watching his step as the trail was slippery.

As the sun was now very deep into the last valley, it was hard to see the trail ahead. Joe wished that he could only have twenty more minutes, he would be home.

The moon was in the last quarter and therefore not much help. The weather was starting to turn bad with the clouds building fast over the mountain tops. Joe knew that he must cover the last half mile quickly.

As he stepped off the trail to check the tenth trap in the series, he again heard a sound very close to what he and Earl were investigating before starting the trail. He knew that it was going to be very dark soon so he kept his concentration on the trap he was looking for.

The location of the trap was disturbed as was the first one. He approached slowly only to see the trap missing. There were some rather unusual looking footprints around the area where the trap was supposed to have been.

As he started to back out of the narrow path leading to the trap area, he heard a loud screech coming from the east side. That was also the direction in which he needed to be traveling.

There were two more traps, between him and the cabin. He quickened his pace and kept looking at both sides of the trail for any possible disturbance signs.

Earl was at the cabin waiting for Joe to return. Where could that kid be? He started to get a bit nervous as darkness fell faster and knowing that Joe would not have a source of light with him. They had discussed carrying flashlights, but that would only mean more weight and that would be unnecessary.

Earl looked for the flashlight. Before leaving the house, he checked to see if the flashlight had good batteries. After all, he may be out there for a while. Sure enough, the batteries were nearly dead. Where were the new ones? He knew they had some, but where were they when he really needed them.

After searching for a few minutes he found them in the kitchen along with matches and other general items. Quickly replacing the batteries, he started out the door to go up the trail.

But then wondering if Joe would remain on the main trail. After all, he could save several minutes if he took a short cut from the last trap. How could they communicate? Grabbing the whistle off the door post as he left the cabin, he started to blow it as he entered the meadow trail where Joe should be coming.

After several minutes on the trail, Earl heard the noises again from the forest, similar to the ones heard several hours earlier. Earl blew the whistle and listened, he thought he heard Joe responding.

Stopping to get a fix on his response, Earl heard some loud crashing sounds several hundred feet to his left. Crouching low, he looked without the aid of the flashlight. The noise stopped after several seconds and he stood up and turned on his light in the direction of the noise.

Nothing.

Blowing the whistle again, he finally got a firm response from Joe. Hurrying up the trail towards where Joe was coming, he again heard noises from his left. After a minute of a rather fast paced hustle, he seen Joe coming at him as fast as he could in the near dark.

As the two met on the trail, they did not bother to discuss the events going on around them. All they really wanted was to get back to the cabin.

After entering the cabin, they now had time to go over the events of the last several hours. Earl asks "Joe, did you have those sounds all evening?"

Responding, with a firm "no" Joe stated "Only in the area of trap two and one herd of spooked deer. Not again until trap ten. There were some markings in the area of a couple traps, odd footprints and one trap missing."

"Was the trap missing or just sprung?" Earl asked.

"Missing" Joe replied.

What had started out to be a rather slow afternoon, turned into a trying evening. Both of them wanted to just sit down and relax for a moment. But they had to put things away and prepare for the trap check in the early morning.

Neither of them really had the heart to prepare food, but they knew that food had to be prepared.

Thank goodness for the microwave. It wouldn't take long for a couple of hot dogs or maybe a prepared dinner in the oven.

Discussing what should be on the menu was not important to either of them. They started to look for causes and reasons.

What were those sounds they had been hearing? Where were they coming from? What had disturbed the ground around the traps on the mountain trails? When would they get the answers?

Joe was a nervous basket case. He had been on the trail several hours and seen all the strange signs and heard the sounds.

Earl had not heard anything except for the early afternoon sounds and then whatever it was while looking for Joe. As Joe started to talk about the ordeal, Earl told him to just relax for a moment.

Joe looked at him and wondered how he could relax when he had been out there in that ordeal and even after dark. Would they want to go separately on the morning trail check?

Earl decided that he would prepare microwave dinners. They would not take long and would not have dishes to clean after. Earl put together two hot dishes for them and sat down to eat.

Not a word was spoken while they consumed their food. As they finished the meal, the wind started to blow briskly. Earl stated, "I will close the Meadow windows, you close the south windows."

They stood up to go close the windows and prepare to turn in for the night. As Earl closed the last window, he thought he could hear something in the meadow.

Not again, he thought. This would certainly be a day to remember. He went to the cabin door and turned on the large spot light that was facing in the direction of the meadow.

As far as the light was effective, he could not see anything. Better lock the doors and make sure the rifle was available in his room. Should he inform Joe that he had heard something and was going to have the rifle ready. He thought it best not to tell Joe, as he had already had a rough day.

After Joe went into his room, Earl picked up the rifle and took it into his room. Looking out the window, watching the grass sway in the stiff wind, he went back to the front door to turn off the spot light.

Just as he turned off the light, there was a brilliant flash of light followed closely by a sharp rumble of thunder. Must have struck close to the cabin, Earl thought.

Now, to add to all the other events of the day, Earl thought about having to get to sleep with thunder. He could close the shudder on the window and block the lightning, but not the thunder. Many of those types of rumbles and neither of them would sleep.

Joe came out of his room and asked, "What does the weather look like?" He did not get any indication of bad weather earlier in the evening. There were a few fast building clouds over the mountains, but that was beyond the meadow and normally did not bother the cabin area.

Earl looked out the window and noticed that the clouds had broken and the thin sliced moon was starting to break through the clouds. Where did that thunder come from only a few minutes earlier?

As Earl turned back to face Joe, he noticed that Joe looked a bit worried. Reassuring Joe was not going to be easy now.

Providing a quick weather report was easy. Earl simply stated, "The moon is now breaking out and clouds getting thin, don't understand where the lightning and thunder came from." That only served to raise Joe's interest level.

As Earl attempted to settle Joe, he knew that Joe was not going to get much rest overnight. He turned on the radio only to have a lot of static. Was the radio station off the air, or were there gremlins in the air also.

Well, maybe they had better turn on the emergency radio and see what was being said in the outside world. It was not good to be in the cabin and no radio.

Especially after the day they had just went through. Joe did not want to listen to any news, he just wanted to get some sleep. He had had enough excitement for one day. Turning to go toward his room, he slowly mumbles "good night" and disappeared into his room.

Earl in the meantime, returned to the front door to look one last time. He just could not get all those sounds out of his mind. Talking to himself, Earl questioned, "What had happen to the traps that Joe talked about?" "What was the cause of all the noises they had been looking for?"

Opening the door, he could see the crescent of the moon in its small glory. The clouds had gone, the wind had settled and now things looked good.

What a strange turn of events. Oh well, time to get some sleep and be ready for the morning. They would have several hours to look over the meadow and investigate the possible lightning strike.

Closing and locking the door, there was a serious quietness in the house. It was almost too quiet. Had the day turned completely around now and gone to the opposite extreme.

Would it now be too quiet for him to be able to sleep? Well, into the room and give it a try. Earl placed the rifle close to his bed just in case.

As he slowly moved into the bed, he could hear the sound of the lonely whippoorwill. Only one tonight, was something wrong in their world also. Earl was at least content to have the one outside breaking up the silence. After all, one happy bird was better than that spooked herd of deer Joe encountered earlier.

Earl was hoping that Joe would at least get some rest. After all, the weather had cleared, the moon was now out and the wind had ceased. Waiting a few minutes Earl went in to check on Joe only to find him sitting on the bedside watching the window.

It was approaching midnight now, they had to get some sleep, for they had to be ready to return to the trails by six in the morning. "Joe," Earl called, "you should really try and get some sleep." Earl tried to convince Joe to count the number of whippoorwill calls he heard and imagine where the bird was.

Joe responded, "There is one bird missing, they are usually in pairs."

Soon Joe layed down and closed his eyes and said he had better things to do than count bird calls.

Five thirty came early for the two. They were dragging their bodies out when they noticed that it was going to be a bright sunny day.

Opening the shudders all the way, Earl took a special look at the mountains on the East side. They had a certain amount of brilliance about them. Stepping out the door there was a fresh smell in the air of the approaching season.

The smell in the air meant that they only had another week to spend in the cabin, their summers work was almost finished. Breakfast was a quick bowl of cold cereal. They had to set trail soon to stay on schedule.

After breakfast, Joe asked Earl, "Should I take a replacement trap along?"

"Yes," stated Earl, "We do not want to loose out on any of those little critters do we?"

They discussed the upcoming days events and left for their respective trails. Joe had the mountain trail again, so he was anxious to see what the hill looked like after all those events the night before.

Earl was a bit jealous as he wanted to see the evidence himself. Well maybe after they returned they would go into the forest and look for signs.

Joe was eager to look over the area and replace the missing trap. He started up the hill and quickly was out of sight of the cabin and could no longer hear Earl attempting to sing his country hill side songs.

As Joe went deeper into the forest, he was constantly looking for signs. How did all those sounds come from such a peaceful forest? He had never had such an eventful night as the last one.

He was so involved in his thoughts that he almost missed his trail signs to turn up into the mountain passes. He started thinking that he had better pay more attention to his trail or he would be in the next trapper's zone.

As Earl sang his way down the hill to the river bottom, he noticed several herds of deer and some new rubbings on several trees. Strange time of year for rubbings. Was he going to pick up where Joe left off the night before? He hoped not.

Well, at least he could see what was going on around him. Half way to the river he came to an area that was partially washed out. That wasn't this way last night he thought. "It did not rain that hard or long for this kind of a wash out." Earl stated out loud.

Earl could now walk around the area without loseing any time. As he walked towards his left, he could now see clearly what caused the wash out. Actually, it was the high winds that were blowing just before midnight and several trees had fallen causing a small land slide.

As Earl reached the river bottom, he again saw several beavers playing, pushing sticks around and getting them ready for winter storage. He figured the beavers had a good handle on the coming season. "Hey beavers, when will the first snow fall this winter?" he ask.

The beavers knew when to get ready for the big change. But for now, time to leave the beavers again and check some traps. He took another look at the river, it was up several feet. Where did all the water come from. There was not that much rain, must have really poured upstream.

He now became concerned about those areas where the water was normally close to the trail and he had to negotiate those logs. He may have to deviate and that would take about twenty minutes of detour for each backwater area. Maybe an extra hour before returning to the cabin. Well, maybe it would be Joe's turn to come looking for him.

When Joe reached the top of the mountain, he looked with awe at the splender of the mountain peaks, some even had what appeared to be a fresh coat of snow.

He looked in every direction at the beauty of the valleys around him. He could just spend the day here. Forget the traps. But duty did call. He must start down the trail before Earl missed him again and started another search.

Looking over the trail as he descended the mountain, he was constantly reminded of how nature works, especially in the mountains. He knew just why he was doing this for the summer.

Checking the first trap and removing the critter, he carefully reset the trap and proceeded to the second trap. The area did not look as bad as it appeared the night before.

Maybe he had gotten excited because of the noises and over reacted. Well, maybe trap two will shed some light on his feelings. As he approached trap two, he could see the area with all the marks. No, he had not over reacted, he was sure of that.

The trap was reset and he continued his route. As he approached the steep narrow area he took time to notice that several small trees had blown over and crossed the trail. It will only take a minute to remove them.

He took the time to clear the trail and continued downward. Why hadn't he noticed the beauty of this side of the mountain before. Joe studied the trail carefully for further marks and possible evidence from the night before.

Approaching the bend in the river trail, Earl could now see the water level on the backwaters he had to go around. "Good thing we didn't put a trap close to the water level, It would not be reachable at this moment," he stated to some passing ducks.

Knowing that he would not be able to cross the fallen tree trail, he decided to depart the trail early and go around the backwaters, he did not need this delay. But there was a trap on the other side of the backwaters so he had to stay close and do it quickly.

There was not much of a trail around the backwaters as the river was not known for its high waters. As he picked his way through the rough wooded, rocky area, he could hear many birds and a few squirrels chattering.

A rather happy morning for them he thought. Soon he was back on the original trail and at the trap. Everything was good here, time to move on. Earl wanted to stop and watch birds and squirrels, but he knew he had several more delays ahead with the river water as high as it was.

As he finished the last of the backwater delays, he started up the final hill towards the cabin. Only an hour late now, "I wonder if Joe will be looking for me?" Earl asked himself.

Earl blew his whistle several times to try and get a response from Joe, if he was out there. Listening carefully, he soon got the impression he was the only one in the woods. Well, maybe in another ten minutes he would blow it again.

When Joe returned to the cabin only a few minutes late, he knew Earl would not be back yet, he settled down in his lawn chair to watch the sun and mountain effects. Peaceful, beautiful, great views, why not relax and enjoy them.

Sipping a fresh cup he settled into the chair in a fully relaxed mood. Figuring he would give Earl about a half hour then he would blow his whistle to start the communication process and go down the trail. Joe was soon asleep in the chair. His cup was sitting in the sun when Earl finally arrived at the cabin.

Earl was a bit frustrated that Joe had not come out looking for him. After all, he was looking for Joe last night. As he approached the chair where Joe was sleeping, he thought about kicking it to wake him up. That would teach him a lesson in thoughtfulness.

Remembering his tension from the night before, he slowly walked past Joe and into the cabin. Making a cup for himself, he went outside and set in the hammock and then stretched out.

He knew he had several hours to relax and then back on the trail again. It did not take long for Earl to be asleep also. Both men now asleep in the late morning sun.

By early afternoon, they were abruptly awakened by the sound of a vehicle coming up the old trail.

Who would be here now, thought Joe. Relief is not due for at least another week.

As they stood up, Joe suddenly realized that he was in terrible pain, sun burn. Earl was not too bad as he was under the tree.

The fall leaves had protected him for the most part. As they intently looked down the narrow trail, watching, they knew it had to be news from the valley floor. Only when there was important news, would someone even attempt to drive up the trail.

Shortly, there was several motorcycles on the scene. As the operators removed their helmets, the two recognized the drivers. They were the people from the research group coming up to see how things were going.

As Joe and Earl related the stories from the night before, they realized they had been set up. The relief group had drove up part way the day before, parked their bikes and set out to spook the boys.

Bill, the team chief, indicated that they had parked the motorcycles just down the trail. Just inside the forest, they had stashed several remote control voice boxes.

They could control them from several hundred feet away. What about the trails, well, they had been there too, they had some rather large cumbersome looking pieces that they made foot prints of.

What about the lightning. Well, that was not planned. "We had wanted to wait until you guys were asleep and then move into the meadow with several wired roman candles. However, as we were stashing them preparing to take them down to the meadow, several of the candles came loose and rolled into the small campfire."

"Needless to say, we evacuated the camp in a hurry, leaving the candles behind. When they exploded, they illuminated the entire sky with one big bright flash. The rest is history," Bill stated.

BAKER'S LANDING

Deep into the mountain valley one after noon there was a feeling that something was not quite right. Earl turned to Joe and asked, "Joe, do you have the feeling that there is something wrong nearby? Something that seems to be apparent and yet not obvious to us? I have a feeling that we should go to the ridge and look things over.

"Earl, all I feel is the very heavy air that we do not usually have to put up with here in the valley. I also think that we should go out and check out the conditions" Joe replied.

As the two picked up the radio and other necessary equipment they carry with them every time they are out, they get a call on the radio. "Hideaway . . . ." a broken voice come over the radio.

"Curl One, this is Hideaway One, are you trying to reach this location?" Earl asked over the radio. Waiting a minute, he repeats the call, "Curl One, Curl One, this is Hideaway One, are you trying to reach this location?"

"Curl One, this is Hideaway One, we are going to Thistle Plateau for a check of the area. We seem to have feelings that something is not right. Can you confirm?" Earl asked the base camp. As they started out the forest trail, they again heard the radio, "Hideaway One, this is Curl One, do you copy?"

"Roger, Curl One, We copy." Earl answered.

"Hideaway One, understand you are leaving camp and going to Thistle Plateau. We know of nothing in the area, please confirm when you arrive at Thistle Point."

"That is a Roger, Curl One, we will acknowledge when we get to Thistle Point" Earl confirmed with base camp.

As the two walked out of the valley and into the large meadow that shares it's serene beauty with Thistle Point, Earl looked out over the vast expanse of the meadow.

"How could anything go wrong in a place so peaceful as this?" Earl commented to Joe.

"Well, it must be something serious in order for us to notice it and not have had any preliminary reports from base" Joe returned the comment. "We have been here several times before, and nothing like this has ever gotten to both of us at the same time."

As they reached Thistle Point, they looked over the large mountain valley below them. There didn't appear to be anything out there. Earl took the radio in hand "Curl One, this is Hideaway One, we are at Thistle Point, there doesn't appear to be anything in this area, do you have any information for us?"

"Hideaway One, there is a report but we are not at liberty to report it over the radio. Please return to your camp, we will have a message sent to your camp. Do you read, return to camp?" Curl One reported.

"Roger, Curl One, we will report to our camp, can you tell us anything at all, such as what, where, danger involved. We are interested to get as much information as possible? Please tell us something!" Earl insisted.

"Hideaway One, all we are going to say at this time is return to camp! We will have a team to your location as soon as possible. For now, return to base and stay by the radio. Do you copy?" came emphatic instructions.

"Roger, Curl One, return to base and standby the radio. We are on our way, it will take us about an hour to get there." Earl replied.

They decided to take the long way home to camp. That would take them past the small river and up Fjord Canyon to the camp.

Taking their time to look in every direction when they came to another bend in the trail, they were not in any big hurry to get to camp.

"Earl, what do you suspect it might be, that they cannot tell us, but will leave us up here? Seems like it is double talk, they don't tell us anything, but yet will send a message to us?" Joe questioned.

As they rounded one of the sharp uphill turns, they come face to face with a black bear and two cubs. Earl threw his hand out as if to tell Joe to stop.

Turning slowly, he signals to Joe that there was an animal ahead of them. Motioning to Joe to back track and get out of there.

One thing they did not want was to confront a female black bear with her cubs at that time of day. Not that any time of day was good to meet that combination.

After retreating to the safety of the corner, they contemplated on how to get around the bear family. Knowing that if they went back to Thistle Point, it would make them late. They needed to get around the bear quickly.

"Earl, There is the small trail about ten minutes up the hill from here, we could take that one. It will be a little steep, but we can try it" Joe reminded Earl.

"Good idea," Earl replied. "We need to get around this spot up front, does that trail return to this one up ahead?"

"Yea, but is quicker from that trail to go straight up the hill to the next ridge, we can cross it and be home sooner." Joe told Earl.

"Let's get on the way, we need to make up time, but we really do not need to be in any big hurry, we cannot go anywhere when we do get there." Earl stated.

As the two started to climb the steep trail the radio sounded off. "Hideaway One, What is your location? Are you anywhere near your camp?"

"Curl One, this is Hideaway One, We had to change trails on the way up the hillside, a family of hungry black bear. We are currently about half way to the camp. Figure we will be there about two thirty." Earl informed Curl One.

"Hideaway One, when you get to your camp, break camp then proceed to LZ 33. We will attempt to have a bird pick you up from that location, do you copy?"

"Curl One, What is going on, you are not telling us something? We understand, report to LZ 33, what time do you want us there?" Earl asked.

"Let us know when you arrive at your camp, we will set an ETA at that time. In the meantime, keep away from the hungry bears and keep moving up the hill.

"Curl One, are we in any danger at this time?" Earl insisted.

"Hideaway One, you will be if you keep asking me questions, right now you are not in any danger, we just need to move you tonight" Curl One stated.

With that bit of information, they continued up the trail. Joe was leading the way now as he was more familiar with it. As they came into view of their camp, they could see that something had been there. Stopping, they surveyed the area closely, looking for any signs of possible human or animal.

Something had rearranged part of the front yard of the cabin. As they approached the front of the cabin, they could see the front door had been broken in. Stopping short of coming into full view of the cabin they wanted to talk again to base camp.

"Curl One, this is Hideaway One, we have had company at our camp, maybe still there. The furniture in front is rearranged and the door is open. What can you tell us now?" Earl asked.

"Hideaway One, can you by pass the cabin and get to LZ 33 or can you return to Thistle Point easier?" they were questioned.

"Curl One, we can't get to LZ 33 from here without passing the cabin, but we can get to Thistle Point. It will take us about twenty minutes to get there. What do you suggest?" Earl asked.

"Hideaway One, go to Thistle Point and wait, we will have the bird meet you there, do you copy" Earl was told by the voice on the radio.

"Roger, Curl One, we copy, but what is going on?" Earl quizzed.

"Hideaway One, just get to the Point, we can talk there. Do not go to the cabin, return directly to the Point, Do you understand?" they were instructed.

"Roger, Curl One, we are moving at this time. Will there be any further instruction at this moment?" Earl said sarcastically.

"Hideaway One, you will understand once we remove you from that mountain. We just cannot tell you much now. We just want you out of there" the command voice stated.

"Curl One, we will be at the Point in less than twenty minutes. We will be at the point waiting for this special bird." Earl stated.

As they moved down the hill, there was great curiosity in the two. They were wondering what could have been so important as to drive them off the mountain. Earl had not been moved off a site in over fifteen years of research.

Just before reaching the Point, they get another call. "Hideaway One, this is Curl One, What is your location?"

"Curl One, we are about two minutes from the designated point. What can we do now?" Earl questioned.

"Well, Hideaway one, We are asking you to get down below the point, get comfortable, we are not going to be able to get the chopper up to your location. In the morning, proceed to DZ 22. We will try that and see if you can get out of there" came more instructions.

"Curl One, We will set up camp under the Point, will that be all right? Or should we proceed toward DZ 22 tonight. We still have several hours we can move." Earl asked again.

"Hideaway One, If you can get down further, that would be better. We do not want you to get to DZ 22 tonight. Plan on being there about ten hundred in the morning. Small bird will make a drop for you folks, you will have to come out the creative way" Curl One instructed.

"Curl One, are you telling us that we are going to have to fly out of here?" Earl questioned excitedly.

"Hideaway One, you will have to assemble in the morning. You will have only a few minutes to assemble and get out of there. Once we drop, the chopper will have to get out of there. You are on your own at that time. We do have help coming, but it will be morning before anyone can get there" Curl One related.

"OK, Curl One, we are going to continue down for a while, but will not get to DZ 22 tonight. Sure wish you could tell us what is behind us, we feel like we are being tracked. How do we know that we are not being followed?" Earl quizzed.

"If you have moved as told, you will be all right. We just want to put as much room between you and camp as possible for the night. You are not in any immediate danger tonight. Just keep moving for now. Let us know when you stop, but in no circumstances will you go directly to DZ 22 tonight." Curl One stated strongly.

Slowly the two moved around the Point and start down a rather steep trail toward DZ 22. Earl was now leading as he had the radio and knew the trail. As they reached the last of several small level spots they questioned themselves as to whether or not they should stay or keep going. Deciding to keep going they thought they would put as much distance between them and the cabin as possible.

As they reached a point about twenty minutes from the designated drop zone (DZ 22) they stopped at a small level spot where they could set up what little shelter they had. After all, they did not leave camp planning to spend the night on the mountain side.

As they set up camp, they heard the wind starting to blow. "Well, a little cover from nature," Joe said jokingly. "We may need all the help we can get tonight."

After setting up camp, Earl took the radio and called,

"Curl One, Curl One, this is Hideaway One, How do you read?"

"Hideaway One, this is Curl One, what is you location?"

"We are at twenty to DZ 22, Curl One, we are ready to spend the night here unless you have an update for us." Earl reported to Curl One.

"Hideaway One, do you have camp set up yet? If so that is all right, if not, we want you to move down to the DZ" Curl One asked.

"Curl One, we have camp set up. If you are thinking of dropping the wings tonight, forget it, very windy here and not a good time of night to fly away. We should have better luck in the morning." Earl informed Curl One.

"OK Hideaway One, please standby for further information about twenty minutes from now. Please be ready to copy information at that time."

"Roger, Hideaway One out for now." Earl replied.

Earl and Joe had to eat survival food as they did not have any other with them. "Sometimes when I eat this stuff" Joe joked, "I feel like a squirrel. All we really need to do is place it on the ground so as to find it and enjoy. We should have packed a few of those crunchy bars in a bag before we left camp."

Returning his joke, Earl replied, "Well, if you want to eat like a squirrel, put it on the ground and play like one. I am hungry enough to go squirrel hunting and may find your food. In the meantime, try and figure out what is going on at our camp. Why are we out here in the woods tonight and not in our cabin."

Shortly, Curl One was back on the air and ready to give information.

"Hideaway One, are you ready to copy?"

"Ready" replied Earl, "Give it to me slowly to give me time to write it down."

"Hideaway One, when you wake in the morning, please inform us. Try and be up and about by 0600. Let us know what the weather is like and we can make firm plans to get you guys out of there. Local weather report from here says it should be good in the morning for the drop. We would like to drop about 0730 so as to get all aspects in motion as soon as possible" Curl one commented.

"Hideaway One, we will talk to you in the morning" Curl One closed the conversation.

Both men had trouble sleeping, with Earl counting the lonesome call of the whippoorwill. At least something was peaceful. As long as the whippoorwill was calling, there was no critter moving around.

About midnight, as the thin moon was disappearing behind the mountain top Earl finally slipped into a sound sleep. He could not count any more calls.

At five thirty in the morning, Joe's watch alarm sounded, waking both men.

"Well, better check camp and see if we have been carried away," Joe said. "After all, there was supposed to have been something up on our mountain to take us away."

Earl looked at him with a half grin, "What is the matter with your attitude indicator, Joe, is it broken?"

Joe looked at him and did not say a word, looks alone were enough to say what Joe intended to say.

At 0600, Earl picked up the radio, calling, "Curl One, this is Hideaway One, We are up and about, what will be our next instruction? Should we move into the DZ and wait for the birds? What will be your ETA to DZ 22?"

"Hideaway One, there has been a change of plans, we need to move you down further if you can. We need to have you get down to the 6,000 foot level. You are above our operating altitude for the drop. That means you will have to go down to the cabin on Mirror Lake. However, before you report into the cabin, please contact us again. How long do you think it will take for you to get down there?" Curl One asked.

"Should take about two hours from where we are now, Curl One. Do you want us to take the most direct route or should we follow the regular trail?" Earl asked.

"Take the lesser used trail, less chance of being followed. It will give us a chance to be at the cabin to meet you" continued Curl One.

"Curl One, what do you mean, less chance of being followed?" Earl responded. "Are we being watched from above and that is why you cannot bring in the birds?"

"That is a negative, Hideaway One, I did not mean to alarm you. That one was not to have come out that way. Just take the lesser trail and we will get you about 1030. Don't be late, we don't like to be kept waiting" said Curl One.

"We will check the cabin before entering and let you know when we are there." Earl said.

As the two men again started down the trail, they were confronted with a female bear and one cub.

"Better find another route fast," Joe responded quickly. "This one looks like she really means business about protecting her young."

Once again faced with an alternate route, a delay in plans, Earl quickly decided to retrace their steps and go back to where they started the day. Taking another trail, they would now be in the area of the cabin about 0930 instead of 0900 as planned. He informed Curl One of the delay and moved down the trail.

As they approached the cabin on Mirror Lake, they could see a sedan setting in front. Better call Curl One and see if it is clear to approach the cabin, Earl thought to himself.

"Curl One, This is Hideaway One, we are in view of the cabin and see that there is a sedan in front, is that for us?" Earl asked.

"Hideaway One, stay away from the cabin, we do not have a car in the area. In fact, please proceed down to Baker's Landing. That should be a good spot for you folks to spend your lunch time. By then we will have the next plan worked out. Do you copy?" Curl One instructed.

"Roger, Curl One, we copy." Earl said with a sort of rejection in his voice.

Working their way around the meadow they arrive at a trail that would take them to Bakers Landing. Arriving at Bakers Landing about 1130, Earl again calls, "Curl One, this is Hideaway One, we are at Baker's Landing, standing in the woods, there are fisherman out there on the lake, people around the shore line, and it looks like the same sedan we seen at the cabin at Mirror Lake setting here now."

"Hideaway One, please keep a very low profile, we don't want to be seen passing through the area. Go South around the cabin until you reach the discharge end and small stream. Follow the stream until you come into the confluence of the Razor Creek and Mirror Creek. Stay there until you hear from us. How long do you think that will take?" Curl One asked again.

"Not more than a half hour if you don't give us more details and don'ts!" Earl answered.

As the two again started out to bypass yet another point, Joe speaks out, "What in the world do you think is going on, Earl? They have been jerking us around all night. I suppose there is a real good reason for all this but it sure doesn't make sense to me. We haven't heard any emergency of any kind, no aircraft in the air, our cabin open, can't stay here or there. It seems to be a real test of our ability to conform to their games."

Carefully they depart the edge of the woods and slip back into cover of the forest. They work their way around the meadow and start toward the confluence. Slowly they work their way through some marshes being careful not to disturb any more of nature than necessary. After all, if they were being followed, they would not want to leave much of a trail.

Reentering the forest they feel they can walk a little faster and cover some real ground as they had been going slowly.

As the two approached the confluence of the two creeks. they decided to call in to report their location.

"Curl One, this is Hideaway One, we are at the confluence, please give us further instructions so we can proceed." Earl inquired.

"Hideaway One, take a break and stay put. We are working on another plan at this moment. Do not enter the area, we are not sure about what is there. Will you have enough provisions for the afternoon? We still have to make arrangements to meet you later today. Don't start any fires, lay low and keep the conversations to a minimum. We will have you out of there this afternoon" Curl One stated emphatically.

"OK Curl One." Earl responded.

The afternoon seemed to pass very slowly for Joe. He wanted to get up and run out of the forest. But he knew his assignment was to keep low and wait. Joe wanted to tell a few jokes but also knew that they were told to keep it quiet. What an interesting situation, all they needed was another bear to come along with her cubs.

Having lunch of a few dry crackers and dried meat, they settle in for the expected several hours. Joe wants to sleep but he knows he should stay awake. He fights back the urge to catch a wink. He finally stands up and stretches, looking over the bank at the confluence.

Watching several beavers working on their new log home. He lays on the bank watching them hard at work. Well, at least someone is working at what is expected of them, he thought. Earl in the meantime was busy taking notes of the events that happened. He noted that Joe had gone to the bank to watch the critters busy at work. Noting how Joe was reacting to all this changing of plans.

Soon enough, the radio again came to life. "Hideaway One, this is Curl One, what is your position?"

"Curl One, we are about 200 feet from the confluence, upstream on the Mirror creek side. We are observing several beavers waiting for your call, thank you." Earl responded.

"Hideaway One, we have good news for you, all is clear on the hill. You can now either return to the cabin or come on out and we will return you to the cabin on the mountain" Curl One instructed.

Joe quickly returned to the radio so he could better understand the conversation. Joe looked at Earl and shook his head.

"Curl One, what do you think we should do, I would like to return to the cabin as soon as possible." Earl said. "We are only several plateaus away from the cabin. We could be there before dark tonight, do you confirm?" Earl asked.

"Hideaway One, you can proceed back up the mountain, stop by the Baker's Landing and get some lunch, take along a

small bite for the trail. You folks deserve to have a party tonight"
suggested Curl One.

Approaching the cabin on Baker's Landing carefully, they see
several people standing around outside the main door. Coming
closer, they see that there are also more people inside the building.
They also see a helicopter setting behind the building. Must have
been what they heard earlier in the day when they were at Mirror
Lake.

Entering the parking lot, they see what appears to be the
sedan that was up at Mirror Lake and also in the parking lot at
Bakers Landing earlier in the day.

As Earl approached the building, he is met by several of the
people that stood outside the building.

"Earl, We have been waiting for you folks to come out of the
woods. We heard you were coming here. Let's step inside and
have a good meal" one man offered.

"Earl, let me introduce myself," said the first to greet them,
"I am Travis Majeski, I am head of security for the organization.
You fellows have just passed one test of tolerance. You will again
be tested sometime down the road. We like to see how you handle
little off beat situations. We have been working on setting you up
for some time. Mr. Millo said you would have no problem with
getting through this test. He has very high standards for you and
Joe," Mr. Majeaki stated.

Joe retorted, "You mean you run us all around that blasted
mountain just to see how we would react. It makes me more mad
now that I know, than I was on the run. I was beginning to feel
like a fugitive."

"Joe, I am Links McGeeh," said a second man. "Lets you and
I go to another table to discuss some possible scenarios that you
fellas will possibly be coming up to in the future. I want to get
your feelings on how they should be handled."

"I don't know if now would be a good time to discuss them,"
Joe commented. "We have just been told that we have been tested
for the last 24 hours and now you want to talk about future
situations."

"Joe, now would be an excellent time as you are still relatively new and learning faster than anyone had ever thought possible. You are almost a light year ahead of most of your contemporaries. We are really happy with your performance. Mr. Millo is very high on you. We need to sit down and just talk. I will keep it light and easy for you. OK" Mr. McGeeh replied.

Joe nodded his head in compliance and followed Mr. McGeeh into the restaurant an took a seat at a corner table.

"So this was all a test? What a work out. I suppose now we have to get ourselves back up the mountain. After all the cabin was open when we last seen it." Joe mumbles to himself.

"Joe, we will get you up the hill in an hour or so. Did you see the chopper sitting out back? That belongs to us and we can get you there in about twenty minutes. We go up and over all those bears you seem to have found on this exercise." Mr. McGeeh comforted Joe.

As they finish their conversation, Earl comes over to Joe's table and nodded his head as if to inquire as to his being ready to go.

"Yes, I think that I have a much better understanding now that we have had this discussion. I now understand the reason for some of the selection processes that we have seen. Why are some people just getting mediocre assignments, we get some very interesting ones." Joe said to Mr. McGeeh.

Joe looks at Earl and grins as he says, "Let's get to the top of the mountain and resume our reason for being up there. I think we can find at least another pair of bear up there somewhere."

As Mr. McGeeh and Majeski lead the two out and around the cabin where the helicopter is parked they see a peaceful sunshine reflecting on the mountain top.

Mr. Majeski gives the helicopter a good once over and then climbs in to start the engine. Mr. McGeeh motions to the two to get inside and strap in. Making his radio calls for flight planning they are airborne in only a minute. "Not much air traffic up here in the mountains." Mr. Majeski comments. "Sometimes we have to wait twenty minutes just to clear the starting pad in Chicago.

This is great flying here, only the up drafts to really be concerned about. There doesn't seem to be anything out here except for beauty."

As they approach the landing area near the cabin, Joe notices that there is someone in the cabin. A stream of smoke coming out of the chimney. "Who did you folks leave in the cabin?"

"Well, I don't think you will mind, there was a volunteer to keep the operation going while you folks took your test. Michelle is watching the place. She volunteered as she wanted to see the mountains from the top. She is really doing well also." Mr. McGeeh commented.

As the helicopter sets down, Michelle comes out of the cabin and moves toward the chopper. As the engine is shut down and the rotors come to a slow spin, she moves up close and enters only after the blades have stopped.

"Heard you boys did all right out there running from the bears. Did you have any more this morning?" She asked.

Joe looked at her with a grin and comments, "Michelle, you should have been the one out there. I have never seen so many bear when I really needed to get somewhere. Seemed as though someone put a bear on every corner for us."

As Joe and Earl get out of the aircraft, they invite Majeski and McGeeh to come in for a spell. They get out and take a look around. "If this is what you folks do a living, I do believe I could learn to like it, especially the locations. Get to come up here often?" Majeski asked them.

"This is one of the lessor liked assignments. You should have seen the one we were at last month." Earl replies. "We were so far up that your helicopter would have had to have aux oxygen to get there. It took us two days to walk in. But the sights and beauty were well worth it. I am hoping to get Michelle up on one of these assignments in the near future.

Mr. Millo is thinking about it, but not committed to letting her in such a place."

"I do think I could take a week or two in a place like this," Michelle came back quickly, "Mr. Majeski if you have any power with Mr. Millo, please tell him I am ready to come back." Michelle almost begged him.

"Well Michelle, I think you are going to have to stop begging us for such an opportunity. You are to stay up here with Joe and Earl for another week. They are going to have to put up with you. But we do have to get going. We will get the extra equipment out of the baggage compartment and let you three spend a week here." Mr. McGeeh stated.

"You mean I am going to spend a week up here? WOW", ! Michelle could not contain her excitement.

As the helicopter lifted off all three wave to the two men and returned to the cabin. Preparing to settle in for a week.

"Michelle, were you in on this test?" Earl asked.

"No, Mr. Millo asked me yesterday morning if I wanted to go to the mountains for a day, he told me to bring along some extra clothing and be prepared to take care of the cabin for a few days if needed. He did not indicate you were being taken out of the cabin for a night. It was kind of spooky here alone last night," Michelle said with lots of excitement.

"OK," Earl said, "let's get you a place set up for the week, welcome aboard and hope you enjoy your week with us."

SOUTH AMERICA

"Joe, can you get in touch with either Earl or Michelle, preferably both of them," Mr. Millo asked.

"Gosh, I don't know, Michelle is somewhere in the mountains of Colorado and Earl is in the islands off Florida," Joe responded. "It could be tough getting either of them, but I will attempt to get in touch with them. What is the urgency?"

"Well if you have been following the latest earthquake situation in South America, we have complications there. It seems as though there is more than just seismic activity going on there. There may also be volcanic activity. We need to study the effects of wild life in the area as soon as possible. The government has asked if we could get someone in there tomorrow. Think we can do it? I have three seats on a flight going that way at 1600 hours," Mr. Millo replied.

"What happens if I cannot get in touch with them? Do I go alone or do you have a backup plan? I am sure you have already thought of a contingency plan," Joe said with a bit of happy sarcasm.

"Well Joe, if you really want to know the alternative, keep me on the phone and you will know tomorrow as you report to the airport," Mr. Millo came back with his charmed wit.

Joe was quick to get the point of how urgent this was and told Mr. Millo, he was on the long distance line as they were speaking and said good bye to him.

Looking for a family telephone number, Joe found a telephone number of one of Michelle's cousins listed on the emergency notification records.

"I will try this one first, maybe she can tell me where Michelle usually retreats to when she goes into the mountains," Joe thought to himself.

"Hello," the phone came to life after only one ring.

"Hello, this is Joe, I am calling from New York, I work with Michelle Leverman on research projects. I need to know where I can get in touch with her if possible. We have an emergency that she would be excellent in handling. Do you know where I can reach her," Joe said with a sense of urgency.

"Well, Michelle is usually here after 6 PM, but we don't expect her back until very late tonight. She is with a group that went out of town. Can I have her call you tomorrow? She will be back about 11 PM tonight," the person on the other end responded.

"Have her call me tonight, I'll give you my telephone number, but I must hear from her tonight. Can you pass it on to her. Tell her the research will involve the area of South America that was recently hit with the earthquake. We need to get in fast and get out of there. Just tell her to call me tonight," Joe almost demanded.

"Well, maybe I can get in touch with the tour operator and they might be able to contact her. But then she will still have to get back here. But I will pass on the message as soon as I can get in touch with the tour company or she returns tonight, this does sound serious," came a strongly concerned reply.

"Thanks, I appreciate anything you can do to get in touch with her. If you are not able to reach her today, please call me tonight yourself. I need to know if she can return to New York and leave about 3 PM tomorrow for South America," Joe almost insisted. "You have my number, please call me."

Satisfied that he could not do any more to reach Michelle, he now went to work trying to find a number he might be able to get in touch with Earl.

"What a time to have two thirds of your best research team on vacation," Joe stated out loud to himself. "Why now, didn't they know this mountain was going to come to life soon. They seem to know everything there is to know about every mountain. Why now of all times," Joe continued.

"Where do I begin, he has several numbers here, someone may know his exact whereabouts. Let me try his parents first, they are generally pretty well informed of his location," Joe started to do his research to find Earl.

After several rings, the voice of a young person answered the phone. "Hello, this is the Charmer residents, may I help you."

"Yes, this is Joe, I work with Earl Charmer on government research projects. Is it possible to talk to one of Earl's parents?" Joe replied "Well, Mr. Charmer is out in the garden, Mrs. Charmer is gone to the store. So I guess it is me you have to talk to. What can I do to help you?" came the positive sounding voice.

Well, I really need to talk to Mr. Charmer. Is it possible to talk to him?" Joe asked.

"No, he is at the far end of the garden and that will take about 10 minutes to get him in here, Can I take a number and have him call you back. I will take the number to him immediately," the friendly voice said.

"All right, it is very important that I talk to him as soon as possible," Joe emphasized. "Here is the number and the time, please get it to him as soon as you can. I really need to get in touch with Earl today."

"Well, why didn't you say you really needed to talk to Earl, he is my big brother, I know where he is at. He is on the Caribbean island of Twyglia. Off the coast of Florida. Do you want to know more," responded the voice quickly.

"Yes, I really need a telephone number where I can reach him, or at least a hotel name. Do you have that much information," Joe ask as if to interrogate.

"Yes, but it will cost you, but I will have to think about the price, in the meantime, I will look up the number for you," came a near demanding answer.

32

"Well, you can almost name your price, I need the telephone number now and we can discuss the amount later" Joe stated.

"Let me have it please. I really need to get in touch with Earl as soon as possible," Joe insisted.

After getting the number, Joe started immediately dialing the number, forgetting first that he needed to get a line access outside the United States. After several attempts, he finally got the number correct and was waiting as the phone was ringing several times.

"Hello, McPhee Hotel, how may I help you?" came the answer.

"I need to get in touch with Earl Charmer, one of your guest," Joe stated quickly.

"Earl Charmer, was in room 555, but checked out last night for the east coast," came the reply.

"Do you have a forwarding number for him, where he might be staying now," Joe stated even more emphatically.

"Mr. Charmer should be in The Blowing Hotel, named that for the fact that the winds are always blowing into the face of the hotel . . ." the desk clerk was explaining.

"That's OK, do you have a telephone number for that hotel," Joe demanded. "I really need to get in touch with Mr. Charmer as soon as possible, not the history of the hotel,"

"OK, I will get it for you, but you don't have to get huffy," came the response.

Getting the new number, Joe quickly dialed it and waited for the answer.

"Hello, this is the Blowing Winds Hotel, How may I help you," came a pleasant voice.

Joe quickly identified himself and the nature of his call. "Yes, we do have him registered as of last night. They came in very late, I don't know if they are in the hotel now or out surfing, came a reply. Let me ring up the room and see for you, one moment please."

"Hello, this is Earl, what is going on that you need to call me while on vacation. I thought I could hide from you," Earl said in a joking manner.

"Earl, I have been on the phone for the last two hours trying to get Michelle and you. I am not in a happy phone mood just now, but here is the situation," Joe commented.

After explaining all the details, Earl quickly consents to giving up the rest of his vacation and return to New York.

"Have you heard from Michelle yet," Earl asked.

"No, but she is on a tour and not expected back until late tonight. We may have to go without her. They may put on another person in her place, sure would like to see Michelle on this one," Joe completed the details.

"It sounds really urgent. I will be on the next available plane," Earl stated.

As Joe completed the conversation with Earl, he hangs up and just sits back for a moment. "Well, now If I can just hear from Michelle within the next few hours we could be off tomorrow."

Just as he was about to doze off, he was startled with the ringing of the phone. "Now who could that be, don't they know I have to keep the phone clear," Joe stated to himself.

"Hello, this is Joe," he stated in an unbusiness like manner.

"Joe, this is Michelle, what in the world is going on. I just got a message over the business phone stating that it was urgent that I get in touch with you," Michelle stated.

"Michelle, we need to be off tomorrow for South America. I can explain everything to you if you can return to New York as soon as possible. Can you do that?" Joe asked with a touch of urgency.

"Joe, I can try and get out of Denver tonight, but first I have to get back to the cabin and get a few things. But I will be on a flight tonight. I hope we can all get together and make this trip. You did get in touch with Earl, didn't you?" Michelle quizzed.

"Yes, he will be in the air with in two hours. Let us know when we can pick you up at Kennedy, Michelle. Where are you at this time?" Joe asked.

"Well, I am somewhere west of Denver deep into the mountains near Vail. I am on the bus, when we get into the next town, I will get off and rent a car to get back to the cabin. From there I will drive to Denver and be on my way," Michelle answered.

"Michelle, call me before you leave Denver and let me know the flight number," Joe demanded.

Finishing that conversation, Joe was now ready to settle down for a short nap. He was just lining up his dreaming mode, he is again awakened by the phone.

"Creepers, can't a man get any sleep around here," Joe commented.

As Joe answers the phone, he knows he is talking to Mr. Millo.

"Yes sir, I have both of them coming back tonight. Michelle is leaving the bus tour as soon as they get into a town with an auto rental and Earl will be flying out within the next two hours. Both will be in New York before midnight. It took some doing, but both of them responded well," Joe informed Mr. Millo.

"Joe, you don't know how important this mission will be. You won't know until you get there. But you folks will be justly rewarded, I promise," said Mr. Millo.

"Well, I will get several hours sleep before I have to pick up Earl and then Michelle will be calling to let me know when she is due in. She is somewhere west of Denver she informs me. It will take a while for her to get back into civilization," Joe tells Mr. Millo.

"Thanks again and get some rest, I will call you about 9 AM in the morning. We will discuss flights at that time, all arrangements are made, just need to wait," Mr. Millo stated.

The morning hours came fast for the three.

About 9:00 AM the telephone rang with all the details of the flight. Leaving New York for Miami. From there, boarding a South American Air Lines aircraft, they are to fly into Bogota. Changing to some small regional airlines and deep into the mountains.

Boarding the Boeing 747 should be routine. Checking in and moving through the terminal as they have done many times before. They almost knew the gate clerks by name.

Arriving in Miami and waiting for the South American Air Lines was interrupted by several demonstrators who tried to stop all flights leaving Miami. Police were everywhere. As they near their planes loading gate, there was trouble also.

Many people refusing to clear the area around the security check stands.

"How in the world did he ever get us on this flight. Why not an American lines with some security," Earl asked without expecting an answer.

"Earl, I think we had better hang back and wait this one out," Michelle stated.

"I think you may be correct on that assumption, Michelle," Joe commented.

After several minutes the airport security had things under control and all were allowed to pass to the aircraft loading gates.

Boarding the aircraft and shortly in the air, they felt relieved just to be out of the airport.

"Just how serious of a problem are we headed into?" Michelle asked with a bit of anticipation.

"Well," Earl said, "we are headed into some uncharted grounds.

We are heading into an area that has not been visited by Americans for a number of years. Missionaries don't even go this far back. We are into a remote area that is very sparsely populated. Should be exciting, the work will be dangerous as there will always be a chance the volcano will blow and we will be close. We can get cut off from the outside world real fast if that happens. Only a few people will know where we are actually going to be."

"We are almost into Bogota, we will have about an hour to change flights there. The regional will actually be our own private flight into the mountains. We will be the only passengers aboard. Then we will have a few native personnel take our gear into the back country. We are supposed to have horses or maybe a helicopter. A helicopter will probably draw to much attention to our location, so bet on a horseback ride," Earl explained to both of them.

As the airplane approached the airport at Bogota, they are alerted that the airfield at Bogota may not be accessible by air because of a storm cell working in the area.

"Great, where does that leave us. We are to meet a connecting flight and probably will miss it because the Pilot cannot land in a storm," Earl complained out loud.

"Well, they will tell us soon where we are going into, cannot go back to Miami now," Joe commented.

"Ladies and gentlemen, this is the captain speaking," came the intercom message, "we are not going to be able to land at Bogota today at all. Instead we will have to divert to Caracas. Sorry for any interruptions you may have to encounter, but there has been a major catastrophe in Columbia and they are not allowing any out of country flights in today. You may be able to transfer tomorrow and fly into Bogota."

After a short moment, there was a stewardess standing at the isle where Joe, Earl and Michelle were discussing their next move. "Excuse me," she spoke in broken English, "which of you are Mr. Charmer?"

"I am Mr. Charmer," Earl spoke up as the other two pointed to him, "What do you need?"

"Well, I need you to come to the forward lounge with me, you have message on telephone. This way please," the stewardess spoke softly.

"Lead the way," Earl spoke again.

"Earl, this is Mr. Millo," We have a slight change of plans as you are well aware of. When you get into Caracas, check in with the Asecho Air Line desk. Do not repeat this message! They will have your further instructions. It appears that the mountain is to dangerous to approach at this time. That is why you are not able to land in Bogota."

"I read you loud and clear, report to the As . . . , whoops and they will provide instructions," Earl confirmed.

"Earl, be careful when you get into the mountain area. You won't have any reaction time if something happens. Always have a backup plan just in case," Mr. Millo advised.

"Thank you, Mr. Millo, that is what every research member wants to hear. We will be very careful when in the area of the mountain. When can we expect to get in that area. Will they tell us at the airport," Earl asked.

"Earl I cannot tell you on the phone, we have said enough for now, keep in touch if you can," Mr. Millo ended the conversation.

"Well, that is enough of that conversation," Earl spoke to himself.

Approaching his seat, he notices several passengers acting rather watchful of their moves. Not wanting to let on that he was aware of their watching, he sat down and had a drink of cola.

"Joe, we have company. Do not look around. Just sit and act as if nothing has changed. We will discuss the future situation later. In the meantime, enjoy your flight to Caracas," Earl informed him. "Pass the word to Michelle that we are being observed and do not get out of sight at any time except to go to the bathroom. The three of us must stick together like we are glued!"

Joe leaned over to Michelle and spoke softly to her. She had a window seat and was enjoying the beautiful sights provided by the evening sunset. Approaching Caracas eventually, nearing darkness, they watched as the airport lights come into sight. Circling East to West over the city, they have a beautiful panoramic view of the mountains and the city.

Upon touch down, Earl carefully points out the two men that he is suspect of.

"They are sitting in seats just forward and across the isle from them. We will hang back and let them exit the plane first. We will stop a stewardess and maybe slip out a side door. We need to make sure that they are not following us," Earl again spoke in a low voice.

With the aircraft stopping and everyone getting up in an effort to be the first one off the aircraft to get connecting flights,

Earl, Joe and Michelle just sit in their seats and let most of the crowd move out.

Stopping a stewardess, Earl ask her for help in getting off the aircraft. She needs to confirm with the aircraft commander what she is able to do.

Shortly, the pilot comes back, "What is the situation, how can I help," he asked.

"Remember the telephone call I had in flight after we were diverted. well, we need to get to Asecho Air Lines without being followed. I have reason to believe that there are two men on board that want to follow us," Earl stated.

"What reason would they want to follow you folks? We have no alert of any potential trouble on the flight. Let me check with the flight people at Asecho, to confirm what you are saying. Stay here for a moment," the pilot informed them.

Returning in a few minutes, he shows concern "Yes, you are being followed apparently. We will take you off through the flight crew exit. That way they will not see you. They will think you have gotten away. What are you being followed for?" asked the pilot.

"A long story," Earl said. "Right now, we just need to get out of here and over to Asecho. Do they have another place for us to meet?" Earl asked.

"Yes, you will meet with them in our lounge at SAA. That is our lounge. No one can find you in there. We will keep traffic to a minimum for you," the pilot suggested.

"Thanks," Earl replied.

Departing the aircraft through the crew exit, they are kept under close security. Moving through the airport to the SAA lounge, they are amazed by the amount of attention they are causing.

"Mr. Charmer, I am Alec Hosea. I work for Asecho and you are to work with me on your situation. I know you are wondering how we are involved. Let's step into the office here and we all can talk," Mr. Hosea spoke startling the three of them.

After going into the office of the SAA vice president, Mr. Hosea turned to Earl and spoke again. "Mr. Charmer, we are going to have to fly you out tonight, but not to your original destination, that being the mountain village. We will take you back to the border where you will spend a day. From there, you will be taken by Colombian personnel to the mountain if you can get there. Do you understand what I am saying?"

"Yes, but now you do add a greater amount of anxiety to this trip, what the heck is going on? We were not prepared for this type of secrecy. When will we know whom we can trust?" Earl asked.

"Well, for beginners, you have to trust me. We of Asecho, are certainly on your side. We have a great deal of interest in your research. Probably should not mention it, but your government is a major sponsor of our airlines. Keep that under your hats. We will all be better off when you have finished your mission. Things will go a lot better. You have a very big responsibility resting on your mission. I know you will do a good job. We were not aware you were being monitored while in the air. Who ever caught on to them must have a very carefully trained eye. We will not discuss how it happened at this time. Others will be interested in your acute observations on the flight," Mr. Hosea said.

"You get us out of here and we won't say a word to anyone. Just make sure that we are not being followed," Earl stated.

"Oh, the two men you observed on the plane, they are being detained by customs, they won't be out of the airport for several hours. We just don't know if there are any more around. This is the safest way. You see, we could not even trust the pilot of the aircraft. We will take you to another aircraft after you have something to eat. Please come this way," Mr. Hosea almost ordered.

After consuming a traditional meal, the three are taken by airport car to another terminal. There they are assisted in loading their gear on board a small twin engine turbo prop for the final leg of their trip to the border. They will spend the night in a small hotel, somewhere.

As the aircraft lifts off, they look back over the wing and observe the city as it quickly goes out of sight.

"That was a bit of strange events," Joe commented.

"Yes, that certainly was strange, we don't often get that type of welcoming committee," Michelle adds.

"Well, we do know for sure now that there is certainly something that is waiting for us on the other end. We should not be surprised with the outcome of this flight. Apparently Mr. Millo was not at liberty to discuss the operations with us. He must have someone on this end who is going to give us our final marching orders," Earl stated.

After the 45 minute flight, the pilot calls back to have the three fasten their seat belts. They are about to land at the border and need to be ready.

"Wonder what will be waiting for us here. We have had enough excitement for one day. I would just like to settle for a safe bed for several hours. Just get us to a hotel," Michelle insisted.

"Touchdown," Earl makes note of the wheels touching down on the runway. "It is so dark out here we cannot see anything. Do you suppose we are so far back that they don't use electricity. I don't even see runway lights now."

As the aircraft taxies up to an old building, they realize that they are in remote country. There are only smudge pots burning to mark the hanger. The plane pulls into the building and shuts down the engines.

"Well you folks have arrived at the end of this part of your flight. In the morning you will be taken to the border and given access to another source of transportation. I do hope you will rest good tonight," the pilot said.

"Well, I guess it must be close to 11 bells by now, probably will not have any difficulty getting to sleep tonight. It may be difficult getting up in the morning however," Joe comments.

"After today, tomorrow should be a snap. We have never had this much excitement getting to a new assignment. This must have been planned very carefully. I don't know how they can improve on this. But at least we should have lost our tails," Earl remarks.

"Yea, let's just get some sleep tonight and see what tomorrow brings. I believe the car is waiting for us," Michelle says pointing to a car sitting outside the door.

As the car pulls up to the hotel, Earl notices a small welcoming committee. "Not again, we have more company."

Getting out of the car, Earl is met with a tall heavy set man sporting a long beard. "You are Mr. Charmer I suspect.

"We have been alerted to the fact you would be here tonight. Sorry you could not get into Bogota. But she lost her head today, meaning the volcano. We will get you into the hotel, make sure you are settled in and meet you at first light. We have a long way to go tomorrow, need all the light we can squeeze out of a day," said the mountain man with near perfect English.

"We certainly would welcome several hours of sleep, this trip has really started off with a full schedule," Earl made it clear they wanted some rest.

Carrying the luggage and equipment into the hotel, they are invited to drop the equipment at the lobby where it will be stored by the group that met them. "You do have to trust us, after all, we have gone through almost as much as you have today. We had to travel by car from Bogota. You see, we were to have met you at the airport and taken off shortly after. We were not expecting to have to travel this distance to meet you," spoke one of the women in the party.

"You mean you had to drive through whatever it was that kept us from landing in Bogota?" Joe asked.

"You got it big guy!" stated one of the other members, "now lets you go to sleep. We must get up early in morning"

About midnight they were all in their rooms, all connected into a long suite. The welcoming party was in the rooms next door.

First light came early for them. With the first knock on the door came a call for early breakfast. Earl moved slowly towards the door to his room, looking out in the hall. Nobody there.

"Where did the little rascal disappear too. He was just beating my door down, now he is gone.

When all were up and ready to go for breakfast, they noticed that the sky was finally showing a sign of light. "When you said early, you really meant it, didn't you?" Joe asked

"We need to be across the Ochee River before 8 AM. If we don't make it, we have to wait until tomorrow. That river gets very ugly after 8 AM," spoke one of the team members.

Crossing the river at just a few minutes before 8 in the morning, Earl noticed that the river seemed peaceful enough.

"What happens to this river at 8 AM that makes it impossible to cross?" he asked.

"About 50 miles upriver, they open a flow control valve, that lets the water out of the reservoir and allows farmers to drain off water they need for crops," said the bearded man.

"We just did make it today. In a few minutes we will be up the mountain where we can look back and you can see for yourself" A woman member spoke.

After crossing the border, they are handed off to an additional team leader. He also has a full beard, but his is much more full. He hasn't seen a razor in many years. Probably spent all his adult life in the jungle, Earl thought.

"Now we will be able to make better time, we won't have to wait for other people to cross highways, bridges or anything, it is open road from here to Casatanaga.

"From there we all go by horse to the mountain pass, there we will go by mule. We will be there tonight if the weather holds up" the new leader said.

"Generally, we get caught in a lot of rain this time of year, but the volcano may have changed all that. You will find out for us, won't you?" said the new leader.

"I guess that may be in the cards, we do not have our full assignment yet," Earl replied.

"Well, we can talk now. We know we are alone. You are to ascend up the mountain and setup instrumentation that will measure how this volcano will affect our rivers and growing patterns. Yes, science can predict, but only you can prove science correct. You will give us the information we need to keep the crops growing, and the harvest coming on a regular basis. No, just in case you think we are dealing in drugs, we are not. We are working on lumber, coffee, and other products that can be grown in the mountains. We have much instrumentation at Casa for you. We may stay there tonight now that the volcano has blown. Things should start cooling down high up soon," said the more senior looking woman on the trail.

"Well, we are here now, take us to the work center, we will do what we can. But one more question, why were those people following us. What are we doing that has them so interested. Is there more than just coffee and trees up here," Earl asked.

"They will not be able to find you here. To much forest, To much real estate to checkout, I will tell you someday. Getting you back out will be much easier, I promise," said the lady.

ATOLLS AHOY

As the steamer approached the harbor in the Atolls, Earl looked out over the vast amount of real estate they were going to be working with. A bit here and a bit there, a lot of water time on this assignment he thought to himself.

"Joe, Michelle, please come up and look at what we are going to be working with," Earl called in the ships radio. "You are missing one of the best approaches of any assignment."

As Joe and Michelle leave the bridge and come down to the deck where Earl was waiting for them, they inform him they were on the deck with the ship's captain, only there could they have a better view.

As the ship comes along the dock and is secured, Earl gets his baggage and books ready to leave the ship. Knowing they were going to be there for several weeks, they were to be prepared with lots of reading and note taking paper.

Michelle grabbed up her luggage and started off the ship. Setting her luggage down as she leaves the ramp, she takes in the beauty of the island, the condition of what she would be working in for several weeks. Was she ready for this type of assignment. She would soon find out, soon the big ship would be gone and there would be no turning back. She would be there if she wanted to be or not.

Joe, in the meantime was taking in the water sights. The water was the color of emeralds, small fish lazily swimming around the dock side. Small peaceful waves lapping at the shore line. He was thinking that he would not be able to contain himself until he was able to get into the water. He was anxious to start the water projects first, regardless of the scheduled sequence. But he also knew that there would be time every day for water works and play. Working in this water was going to be fun for him. What could go wrong on this assignment.

As Earl corralled both of them coming down the dock, he informed them that it would be two days before they would be into the real assignment. There was going to be some preliminary layouts that needed to be completed and test to be conducted before the play in the water could begin.

Earl continued to inform them. "There was the mountain trail that had to be checked and plotted. The results of previous test to be verified. There was the water test that had to be done with the equipment that was on board a small boat due in with in several hours.

"Joe, why don't you take a hike up the willow trail and see if there is anything up there from previous test. Anything that we can use to get started with" Earl stated. "Michelle, you can take a walk along the beach and see if there is any signs of former tests there to start with."

"Earl, do you think it is fair that she goes to the beach alone, why don't I go with her to show her what she is looking for" Joe complained in a joking manner.

"Joe, do you think you know any more what to look for than Michelle, after all, we've all just completed the same orientation program and should have about equal ideas" Earl replied.

"Michelle, do you think you can handle the beach by yourself or do you want some help?" Joe asked.

"Joe, I am a big girl and well trained, why don't you go the hills and look for snipes like you were told" she replied.

"OK, now that we have our initial assignment, I am going into the office and start working on the master approach to this marvelous assignment. We have plenty to do and precious little time to get it all in" Earl comments. "One thing that we must remember, no one goes out on one of the test runs by themselves, there will always be two of us and always two radios in each team. All you are to do now is check the areas, don't try and conduct any experiments by yourselves. We will know when you return if you were trying to do more than just check the areas" Earl informs them to restate some basic rules of the mission.

After setting up creature comforts in the cabin that was to be their home for the time on the island, they study the lay out of the island and trails to be used. Staying on the trails would be important as wandering off them would be dangerous because of previous test conducted many years ago. They were going to have to stay close and pay attention to where they were wandering. Areas of the islands were not safe to be traversed.

"Joe, by the time you get to the hill, the boat should be coming in, you can probably make radio contact with them and let them know we are in and waiting. They are to be bringing in some more needed equipment for us."

"You can return here and then join Michelle on the beach when you make contact with them. Keep me informed of your progress, both of you" Earl directs Joe.

As Michelle starts out the door and down the trail, Joe starts up the hill complaining about him not going to the beach. He feels cheated, not going where he wants to go.

As Michelle approached the beach, she stopped and looked out over the large bay and into the ocean. She is amazed that there is so much open territory and yet so far from anything. She looks over the area of the beach where they will be working. As she walks down one of the trails, she is startled by the crackling of the radio.

"Lagoon One, this is Lagoon Two, do you read?" Joe asked.

"Lagoon Two, this is Lagoon One, how does it look up there?" Earl replied.

"Lagoon One, we have some signs of tampering and some broken equipment here. I do believe we can repair it before the start of the big test, just will take time we hadn't planned on" Joe informed Earl.

"Lagoon Three, Where are you?" Earl asked.

"Lagoon One, Lagoon Three is up off the beach a bit, the trail looks kind of overgrown and may need cleaning before we start. Areas look tampered with here also. We all need to take a look here before we start anything" Michelle responded.

"Lagoon Two and Three, please return to base and let's discuss what you are finding. Joe, try and raise the ship before you return. Keep trying until you get them, we will be off the air so you can have clear frequency" Earl said.

"Lagoon One, this is Lagoon Two, I copy and will try and reach the ship as I come down the hill" Joe complies.

"Swordfish, this is Lagoon Two on the Atoll, do you read" Joe called. "Swordfish this is Lagoon Two on the Atoll, do you Read?"

"Lagoon Two, this is Swordfish, we have a fix on your location, are you really in the Labyrinth Bay area. That is some pretty rough terrain to be working in" a response came back.

"Swordfish, we are indeed in the Labyrinth Bay and are finding some disturbing signs already. When do you expect to arrive at this location?" Joe asked.

"Lagoon Two, If we don't run into any weather, we should be there in two hours. We are running a bit late from last port. Equipment was not ready and therefore had to wait. Any problem with two hours from your point? We could speed up a bit but only gain a few minutes and hard on the boat" Swordfish responded.

"Swordfish, take your time, save the boat, we will be ready for you in two hours. Weather looks good from here, clear sky and not a cloud. We can be ready for you when you arrive and will not delay you very long. What are your intentions after offloading, will you move out quickly or stay for dinner?" Joe asked.

"Lagoon Two, you drive a hard bargain, we would love to stay for dinner, but we would like to clear the Bay before it gets too late and any possible weather comes up. We would like to clear the Atolls before dark. They don't have good weather there very long, so take advantage of it while we can, in and out today, maybe another day when we are passing by" Swordfish came back.

"Roger, Swordfish. We understand and will take a rain check on the dinner" Joe said.

Turning his attention to base camp, he called Earl and informed him of the circumstances, figuring that Michelle would be able to hear the conversation with both the boat and base.

As the hour passed, Joe returned to base, asking "Hey, where is that beach loving girl that took me away from the best assignment I could ever have had."

"Haven't heard from her, she hasn't checked in, call her and see where she may be at this time. She should have checked in half an hour ago, but I got so wrapped up in this planning, I forgot to call her. She should never stay off the air this long" Earl comments.

"Probably laying on the beach taking in the beautiful sunshine, I would be if I were down there" Joe comments with a sun starved look on his face.

"Lagoon Three, this is Lagoon Two, where are you at this time?" Joe calls. "Lagoon Three, this is Lagoon Two, what is your location. Lagoon Three! What is your location?" Joe called again.

"Earl we may have a problem, Michelle is not responding" Joe called in to Earl.

Immediately Earl leaves the table with the planning charts, "What are you saying Joe?" Earl asked. "Are you telling me you cannot get a response from Michelle, let's get down to the beach and check it out now."

"Lagoon Three, this is Lagoon One, do you read?" Earl called.

As Earl and Joe reach the beach area, they can see where Michelle had been, but no sign of her. "Lagoon Three, this is Lagoon One, do you read." Earl shouted into the radio.

"Lagoon One, this is well you know, we have Lagoon Three as you call her. She is OK for now, be we are not sure how long we can say that. We need to know what you Lagoons are doing on the Atolls, this is territory that has been spoken for, you are trespassing, do you understand" a raspy voice responded.

Earl quickly turned to Joe and looked over the beach area. "We don't even know if they can see us now. We may be in their sights, let's get back up closer to the bank and think this through" Earl said with a bit of nervousness.

"Lagoons, Whatever you try and do, remember, we know your movements and also we have one of your Lagoons" came a quick response on the radio.

"Joe, change frequency and call the ship and ask them to hold back. We do not want them here with this mess. Ask them if they know of any swat team or other form of help that can be called in. Have them inform Mr. Millo. He will also start some kind of reaction" Earl instructed Joe.

As Joe changed channels, he takes a slow look around the beach head. He could not see any signs of movement.

"Swordfish, Swordfish, this is Lagoon Two, Please listen carefully. Do you read?" Joe started his radio conversation.

"Please come back on channel eight, repeat, come back on channel eight"

"Lagoon Two, what's up, is there trouble on the Atoll. We know you must have something going if you are calling us on emergency. How can we help?" Swordfish responded.

"Swordfish, we have a big problem, someone has kidnapped one of our workers, a female, and are threatening us. We do not know their location at this time. They have us under observation. Which is possible, there are thousands of places they could be hiding. Please Call Mr. Millo and inform him of the situation. Just do not do it on the standard band radio, we do not know what equipment they have here" Joe informed Swordfish.

"Roger, Lagoon Two, we are on it now, will let you know when we have a potential solution." Swordfish said.

Turning to Earl, he nodded his head and said that help may be on the way but would have to wait and see, Joe told Earl.

"This is Lagoon One, Do you read? Earl Asked.

"Yea Goon One, we read? What is the problem, don't you know how to handle such a situation as this. Maybe you will look around the corners next time you decide to invade private property" came a response.

"This is Lagoon One, what are your intentions with the team member? Please do not harm her. What do you want of us, we are only doing research on the safety of the island? We would like to talk it over with you. Send one of your members out and lets discuss this situation" Earl pleaded.

"Goon One, you have this all wrong, we have the girl, you are listening to us, not the other way around. Remember who is holding who here. Besides, you have a ship coming in with supplies, we need some provisions and equipment that is on that ship" came the response.

"Lagoon One here, Why don't you want to send out one of your people and talk. What harm can it do, you can stand off at a distance if you want" Earl again pleaded.

"Joe, see if you can call the steamer, he may still be within reach. Ask him to return and play a decoy, we know they want provisions and supplies as well as equipment that is to be on Swordfish" Earl spoke softly to Joe.

"Saro Imo, this is Lagoon Two, Atolls Island, channel eight, repeat, channel eight, do you read." Joe called.

"This is Saro Imo, channel eight, Lagoon Two, what is going on, why the emergency radio frequency? please come back," came a response.

"Saro Imo, this is Lagoon Two, we have one member of our team kidnapped by an unknown force, they are holding the girl. They are after our supplies and provisions as well as equipment on the Swordfish. We need help. Can you return to port and help. You are the closest one to our position. We have called Swordfish and ask them to contact HQ. What is the likely hood you could run back and help. We do not know how many are in the hills. They have us under observation so they say" Joe informed the steamer.

"Roger, Lagoon Two, we are turning at this moment. We will need to devise a plan where we can get into port and help any way we can. We just passed a small convoy that may be able to give us some help. Let me see if we can raise the captain of that convoy for help. It could be right down their alley" the steamers captain came back.

"Hey Gooney, We are waiting for a ship to arrive in several hours, where is your ship at this time. They should be coming in soon, right?" came the raspy voice again.

"Could be they have run into some weather out there and are holding out" Earl said. "Let me call them and ask them what their status is."

"Swordfish, this is Lagoon One, what is your status at this time, how is the weather at your location?" Earl called on the standard channel.

"Lagoon One, we are having some foul weather here, it may be several hours before we can make it in, if it gets to dark we will have to wait off shore for daybreak. Too dangerous to come in after dark, I figure we can make a decision within two hours if we can come in tonight, keep that dinner warm for us" the captain responded.

"Roger, Swordfish understand you can make a decision within two hours if you can make it in tonight. Thanks a lot, we will return to our cabin and wait your call" Earl replied.

"Looney One, go back to your cabin and stay there, we will tell you when to come out. We will run things for now. Do you copy?" came a response.

"Joe, they are not very smart, they must know they are broadcasting out to the ship. They must know that the ship can hear them. What do you think they are up to?" Earl asked.

As Earl and Joe start up the trail towards the cabin, they know they are being watched. They know the people holding Michelle are not far away, what do they really want. They did not take Michelle, they just took a person.

Turning his radio down so any transmission would not be heard, Earl instructed Joe to do the same, indiscreetly. They returned to the cabin knowing they were not alone. Only hoping that Michelle would be safe for a while.

"Joe, that steamer captain made an interesting comment, he said something about a convoy and it was their job to help in this type of situation. What do you suppose he was talking about. Do you suppose there are some large gray ships out there with cammy clothing just waiting to go to work?" Earl asked.

"Earl, do you mean what I think you mean, they are out at sea and may be coming in. How will they find us and know who the good guys are?" Joe questioned.

"Joe, if they are even coming, they will know from information gathered from the steamer. They will get information from the Swordfish also. They may come in over the mountain. Let's hope they come in soon." Earl said.

"Lagoon One, this is Saro Imo, we are about two hours out and have a plan, can you talk?" came a call on the radio.

"Saro Imo, this is Lagoon One, yes we can talk." Earl stated.

"Lagoon One, we have a friendly force that does not take to kindly to people kidnapping a young lady. We have informed them of your exact location, try and stay in the cabin if you can. Anything moving outside may be brought to their knees after dark. Repeat, stay in the cabin. Swordfish will stay out at sea around the corner acting like a fishing boat" instructed Saro Imo.

"Roger, Saro Imo, will stay in cabin after dark. Will make contact with the kidnappers before dark to see if Michelle is still OK." Earl replied.

After another hour, Earl stepped outside to communicate with the forces to be and check to see if Michelle was still OK.

Telling them that they were still waiting for the ship and it may have been delayed because of the storm out at sea.

"Understand there is a fishing boat near the back side, not one of their ships, the Swordfish will be coming in from the North. They knew nothing about the fishing boat on the back side of the island." Telling them he was going back inside the cabin to spend the night, and asking, please do not hurt Michelle.

Reentering the cabin, he looked at Joe and shook his head. "What do you think is going to happen?"

"I hope those cammies on board rip them apart after they get Michelle out of there. I wonder if Swordfish was able to get a hold of Mr. Millo. He must have an answer by now. I don't think we can get an answer from them if they are on the back side of the island" Joe mumbles.

"Swordfish, this is Lagoon One, do you read? Earl called.

"Lagoon One, this is Swordfish, we are about 40 miles of shore, we are not the fishing boat behind the island, we are going to meet up with the gray ships and give them a floor plan. They are about twenty miles from us now. We will meet within the hour and pass the information necessary. As the steamer said, stay inside, because it will not be nice outside once they have Michelle safely in their corner" Swordfish responded.

"Roger, Swordfish, we understand, stay in cabin after dark. Seems like that is all you folks out in the water can say, we are finding it a bit nerve raking to just sit and wait. Keep us informed" Earl requested.

"Lagoon One, we have been monitoring the conversation between you and the bad guys, must be nerve raking to be there and not able to help Michelle. I don't understand why they are broadcasting on the radio" Swordfish commented "Talk to them once in a while, we can get a good fix on their location and tell the gray ships where they may find company"

"Swordfish, can you pinpoint their location if we keep talking now and then? I can talk to them now and then to assist if needed" Earl replied.

"Lagoon One, stay in the cabin, don't go outside. Things are going to get interesting soon enough. Just call them every half hour from now and let us work on location. It will be dark within an hour. Help is working and by the way, we have informed Mr. Millo, he concurs with this plan of action."

After half an hour, Earl calls the group to talk to them again, insuring as best he can that Michelle is still OK. He also informs them that they would be off the island if they release Michelle and take the supplies they want in the morning.

"Lagoon One, this is Saro Imo, We will be in port in about twenty minutes, you should be able to see our lights if you come to the top of the little knoll out front. Let your friends know the ship will be able to be boarded about dark. That should take several people off the hill for the forces to work on. Put on some lights on the port so we can see to tie in" the captain stated.

Joe hinted that he would go out and look, but Earl held him back. "Let me call the group first so they will know why I am turning on the harbor lights. They might be a bit nervous when they see a ship come in".

"This is Lagoon One, do you read?" Earl asked.

"Looney, we read, what do you need" came an immediate response. "We have been informed that our ship will be docking in about 20-30 minutes. I am going to turn on the lights so they can see the harbor. If I don't they cannot see the docks to tie in. Don't get nervous when the harbor lights up. Do you understand?" Earl informs the group.

"Yea, Gooney, go ahead and light up the harbor, it would be better to get the equipment after dark anyway. If we get what we want, we will turn this pretty young thing loose and not harm her, what a shame however" came a reply.

As Earl threw a switch to light up the harbor, he could see the effects of the illumination on the horizon.

"Saro Imo, this is Lagoon One, we have the harbor lights on, can you see them?" Earl asked.

"Lagoon One, we can see the lights, stay in the house, you have company all around you. Gray forces have located many of them, as many as thirty, maybe forty. They are coming out of the hills to help off load the ship apparently. This may make it easy for the gray forces. We have some gray forces on board, others are probably approaching the shores about now. Remember, stay inside. Things are going to start popping shortly. There will be a small moon tonight and that will help locate them" the captain stated.

Looking out the window, Joe could see some of the upper mast lights of the ship, coming into the harbor.

"Earl, the big ship is coming into the harbor, soon help will be here. What do you suppose they will do? How long do you think it will take, I am getting a bit nervous now that things are about to happen" Joe confided with Earl.

"Swordfish, this is Saro Imo, what is your position?" came a call on the regular channel.

"Saro Imo, Swordfish is about to dock in, plan to spend the night here. Seas are kind of rough out there" the conversation continued.

Earl soon realized what had happened on the dock, Swordfish and Saro Imo had temporarily changed names so that more cammies could come in. Swordfish was still out at sea somewhere, but the bad guys did not know it.

Shortly after the big ship tied in, it was dark. "Lagoon One, we are docked in and ready to come up for dinner, hope it is still hot" came a radio call.

Earl responded, "Bring your entire crew up for dinner, we have enough for all, We will have a box lunch for the poor crew man who has to stay behind and mind the store. We will off load in the morning".

"Roger, we will secure the ship and leave it in port. There won't be any need to leave a person behind for now. We will return to the ship within two hours anyway. We will be bringing the entire crew. There are only twelve of us. Put on a fresh pot of coffee. It could be a long night for some of us" the radio spoke.

"Bring the whole crew, we are ready" Earl responded.

About a half hour later the crew approached the front door of the cabin.

Opening the door, Earl was relieved to see the men come into the cabin. Now what was the next move. One of the men approached Earl and identified himself as a Seal.

"What are you fellas doing out in the middle of the ocean? Don't answer that, thank you for being here, just get our girl out of there and back to us" Earls voice took on a sense of urgency.

"What are the best plans you have for getting to that point?" a man asked, pointing to a map. "What are the trails like?"

"Here are the best trail maps we have" Earl showed him several maps.

"You fellas stay here, we will have several people outside, and in the area, several in the ship and by now, a lot on shore, stay inside. It could get ugly out there before long. We are working with scopes and other technical weapons, we cannot identify friendly or foe at night, only bodies moving. We will be to the girl soon, we know where she is, we just need to get to her. Most of the people we are looking for are at the ship, we probably have them under control already. They fell for the idea that the entire ship crew came up for dinner" said one of the big men in cammies.

Joe offered coffee to the men remaining in the cabin, but all refused. The ship crew did take small cups of coffee and tried to eat a little. No one was in the mood to eat or discuss the situation, only wish that everything was over and Michelle was out of there.

After what seemed like an eternity, there was a sound outside the door. One of the men dressed in cammies jumped up and slowly approached the door. Listening closely, he slowly opened the door, and there stood several men dressed in cammies holding Michelle.

She runs into the cabin and grabs Earl and Joe, one in each arm.

All three hugged for a long time.

Finally, one of the men spoke up, "We have to be going now. Our ship is coming in and we would not want to miss it. We will take all the culprits with us. You should be all right here now. We have covered the entire mountain, can't find anything moving."

As they start out the door, there was a call on their radio "Seal One, please stay put for the night, storm coming in and we are going to stay out of port tonight. Those folks probably would feel better knowing you were there for the night. We will pick you up in the morning, Gray Ghost here, Out"

As dawn broke over the small atoll Earl looked outside. Surprised, he could see about thirty small clumps, in the area of the cabin. Must be the seals. Where are those bad guys, he wanted to get his hands on them.

Offering all them coffee, he could then see that some of them were already gone from their sleeping places. Some had gone over the hill to check for more people. Only to round up several more. All together, the Navy Seals apprehended forty-six people. Most of them just plain folks who had looked for adventure, not really knowing what they were getting into.

As Joe, Michelle and Earl watch the Navy Seals go down the hill, they could see some of the ships sitting out at sea.

"What an Armada" Michelle commented. "They really took that camp by surprise last night. They really knew just where to go and when to get there. I don't know if I could have been rescued in the morning. The men were starting to talk and make gestures about my being there. Most hadn't seen a woman in several months"

Soon there was another call on the radio. "Lagoon One, I understand it is safe for Swordfish to come in, is that correct?

"Swordfish You are welcome in this port anytime. Come on in and have a cup of coffee" Earl insisted. "This is one crew that is really happy for your cooperation last night. We have recovered our most valuable asset, Michelle, and are ready to get down to work now".

"Lagoon One, We will be in port as soon as Saro Imo, leaves. We have passed the long gray line that provided you with the cammies, last night. I understand they did a great job, not a shot fired, captured a bunch of intruders. You should see the lineup of ships that have stopped just for you folks. There is a lot of gray ships sitting out here waiting for the team players to join them again. They are a great bunch of fellas" Swordfish responded.

"By the way, when we get in, Mr. Millo wants us to take you to the big islands for a day or two of rest. He wants to send in a team to sterilize the place. He knows you will enjoy a couple days in the islands on the real beach. Leave the cabin as is, a team will be in later today to take care of it" the captain informed Earl.

"Joe, Michelle, did you hear that, we get a vacation so that the island can be sterilized. I would like to have seen those Seals in action last night. I would like to have seen the expression on those guys faces when the Seals took them one by one", Earl commented.

I don't ever want to go through that experience again" Michelle stated.

THE SUSTEN

As the radio continued to broadcast storm warnings, Joe and Earl sat by the stove to keep warm. "Where in the world did this storm come from, Earl?" Joe asked.

"Joe, it's not where did the storm come from, but where is Michelle?" Earl countered. "These mountains here in the Susten are no place to be when this type of storm comes up."

"We are not prepared for a couple of days up here at this altitude. But our first concern now is where is Michelle" Earl continued.

"Do you think we will have enough wood for heating over night? What about covering the windows so we can retain some heat we have now?" Joe asked without giving Earl a chance to answer.

"We don't even have spare batteries for the radio, we were not expecting to have to weather a storm here on the Susten. I guess we better be conservative on the usage of the radio also. But we need to keep it on for when Michelle tries to get in touch with us. We need to decide which is best for now." Earl stated with a bit of concern in his voice.

Soon darkness fell over the early summer mountain area. No word from Michelle.

"She will have to be stopped for the night by now, she will not try and travel overnight. She is probably snuggled up against some big old rock or has herself a burrow to stay in. I am glad she took the extra set of warmers with her" Earl commented.

"Think we better turn the radio off now and save the battery?" Joe asked Earl with a shiver in his voice.

"Yea, better turn it off, but first, go out and try and reach her one more time. I would feel better knowing where she is for the night" Earl directed.

Putting on the only heavy coat they had in the cabin, Joe stepped outside and called Michelle over the radio. After trying several times, and shivering even more, Joe stepped back inside the cabin to tell Earl that he was not able to reach Michelle. As he was putting the radio down and ready to turn it off, there was static.

"Wait a minute, Earl, there is someone on the radio. I heard some static, meaning there was somebody using our frequency and trying to respond to our call, I will step back outside and try to hear" Joe said moving toward the door.

Moving out into the snow beyond the cabin, Joe put the radio close to his ear to try and understand what was being said over the radio. The radio only crackled, no understandable message.

"Michelle, If that is you, key the radio one time, If it is somebody else, key it two times" Joe ordered.

Waiting for a response, Joe stood as still as he could while shaking from the cold.

Suddenly there was a series of crackles on the radio. Joe did not know what to think of that. Once again, he called out, "Michelle, if that is you, one key please. If there is someone else out there key two times."

The snow was getting unbearable for Joe, he started back to the cabin when there was one crackle on the radio.

"Michelle!, I heard one key on the radio. One more key if you are in a safe spot for the night" Joe yelled as he ran to the cabin.

"Earl, I have one key on the radio, she must be OK for now. I am waiting for her to respond to make sure" Joe said with great excitement forgetting he was very cold.

Then came two keys on the radio, Joe sank in place when he heard the second key, possibly meaning that Michelle was not safe. Joe called again to Earl, who came out of the cabin to better understand Joe's comments.

"Earl, we may have a problem, I just received two keys on the question of are you safe for the night . . ." Joe said with a bit of concern in his voice.

"Joe, I suggest we make contact with the base and report it to them, they only know we are in a storm, not that Michelle is missing. Then we will try and get back to Michelle, but our batteries will not last another hour in this weather" Earl reminded Joe.

Changing channels on the radio, Joe calls "Susten Base, this is Rocky Point Two, do you read? Susten Base," this is Rocky Point Two, do you read, we have an emergency at this point. One member is out of touch in the storm and we do not have radio contact with her."

"Rocky Point Two, this is Susten Base, restate your situation, repeat, restate your situation, this is Susten Base. Understand may you have a member of your team out in the storm. How bad is the storm?"

"This is Rocky Point Two, Michelle is out in the storm, we cannot receive any messages from her. We do get a bit of static which responds to the question, "Are you safe for the night?, with a negative response, it tells us she is in danger."

"Please advise if you can respond at this time of night? She is in need of help and we only have less than one hour on this battery. Please try and send help up if at all possible. We are currently under about a foot of fresh snow here at the cabin. Will there be any other information you need?" Joe continued to talk.

"Rocky Two, that is not going to be easy, we have storm warnings all the way down here. It will be difficult to get something up there before morning. We will advise the Swiss National authorities and see what they want to do. In the meantime, try and stay in touch with Michelle. We will advise, will call in one five minutes, do you understand?" came the response.

"Susten Base, if she is not in a good spot now, she may not last through the night. We need to try and get to her now, the morning will be to late. Have the Swiss Nationals bring their best to this one. She deserves the best search team they have. Do you understand, will wait for your next call in one five." Joe responded.

"Earl, they don't think they can make it up here tonight. They have storm warnings down there." Joe shouted to Earl.

"Hey, if they only have warnings, that means they can still travel up the mountain, get them back on the radio and try and demand they get something moving now!" Earl demanded. "We were really not prepared for this kind of action."

"Susten Base, this is Rocky Two again, Earl tells me if you only have warnings, that you may still be able to travel. We are in the midst of a deep snow here, but we are going out to try and find her. We have an idea where she should be at, but may be off course because of not being able to follow the trail. Do you read this transmission?" Joe asked.

"Rocky Two, this is Susten Base, DO NOT attempt to go out in the storm, one is enough. Let us try and find a search team that can be assembled at this time of night. It may not be easy. Will call you back again, stay close to the cabin, do you understand?" came the response.

"Roger, Susten Base, understand" Joe replied.

"Joe, We need to try and reach Michelle again. Give it a try, we will go to what is the base of the research area and try, let me put on several more layers of clothes. Wished I had those hiking boots I was looking at. You might want to put on more also." Earl spoke softly to Joe.

"Michelle, this is Rocky Two again, do you still hear my radio, key one time for me, please" Joe asked over the radio.

Pausing for a moment, Joe and Earl stand in nearly waist deep snow.

Then a short bit of static came in on the radio.

"Michelle, are you in danger of not making it through the night?" Earl asked.

Another static reply on the radio.

"Are you on the mountain?" Earl asked

Two bits of static came back.

"Are you on the plateau in the canyon?" Earl questioned
Again two bits of static.

"Michelle, are you in immediate danger at this time?" Earl continued to question.

The reply was a bone chilling single bit of static.

"Joe, we have got to get to her position as soon as possible. We still have about thirty minutes of battery remaining according to the gauge, we will do everything we can to get to her. We are not really prepared to go out in this stuff either" Earl stated.

But I will be darned if I am going to let her go at this alone, she is to precious to us for this kind of deal" Earl stated.

After a few moments, Joe and Earl are prepared as best they can be to travel.

"Rocky Two, this is Susten Base, Do you read me?" came a radio call.

"Susten Base, we need you help as soon as possible, we just got a signal from Michelle that she will not make it through the night without help, she is in immediate danger. What do you have for us?" Joe replied.

"Rocky Two, we have a rescue team assembling at this moment, I will take several hours however to reach your point, can you radio hold out that long. They are coming by road and will be out of here within the half hour. They know the area well" came the reply from Susten Base.

"Base, our radio will only last about a half hour. We are nearly out of power. I do not know how long Michelle can continue to communicate with us. We know how long we have. Please tell them to be careful but get here as soon as possible" Joe stated with a bit of emphatic tone.

"Roger, Rocky, we understand. We will advise you when the team leaves this location. But in the meantime, stay in your cabin." Base replied.

Finishing that conversation, Joe and Earl take a few flares with them and start out across the flats in the back of the cabin. They know that the flares will provide heat as well as light for them in the storm.

"Michelle, Do you know your exact location from the cabin? Are you sure of your location?" Earl asked.

Shortly, there was a static reply.

"Using the one, two, three method, are you north, west or south of the cabin?" Earl asked Michelle.

Pausing again, they wait for a response. After what seemed like an eternity they receive a three on their radio.

"Michelle, that means that you are south of the cabin, is that correct?" Earl asked.

Again a single response.

"Michelle, are you dug in for the night?" Earl questioned. "we only have about twenty minutes of radio left if this gage is even correct in the cold air."

There was no response for a moment. then came two bursts of static.

"Michelle, are you in the mountain pass or closer to the ledges?" Earl questioned.

Then came the dreaded two keys on the radio.

"Michelle, that means you are in the open and on the windy side of the face, is that correct?" Earl inquired.

After a moment, there was a single key on the radio.

"Michelle, there is a Swiss National rescue team being assembled at this time, but it will take them several hours to reach the cabin. We have asked them to get here as soon as possible, but that will not be easy, they have a lot of road to cover to get here. Whatever you do, don't give up, keep fighting. Do you hear me? Earl asked."

There was that one key again, which made Earl feel a little better.

"Michelle, we are working our way to your location, we will have to turn our radio off to save power. We will try and reach Susten Base again before we turn off, please wait and try to build some kind of snow shelter for yourself," Earl informed Michelle.

"Susten Base, this is Rocky One, What is the status of that Rescue team? We have a fix on Rocky Three's position, we believe we know where she may be. But she is not able to communicate, only key her radio. We have her fixed on the South side of the box and on the open ledge area. That may help you better prepare for the search. Please tell me that the rescue team is in transit at this time" Earl almost insisted.

"Rocky One, you were told to stay in your cabin, the rescue team left this location several minutes ago. They figure it will take about one three five to reach your location, depending on the location of that storm. I will give them the information you have just provided us, they can start plotting the area while in transit. For now however, stay in your cabin, it is safest for you, we do not know the snow condition, what about avalanche conditions. We just do not know, stay in the cabin. We have notified New York of the situation, he is waiting for further information" came a reply.

"Susten Base, we are dropping markings as we go along. The rescue team should be able to follow them. We cannot just set in the cabin and wait for one of us to freeze. We are moving toward the flats and the ledge area. Remember those little chemical things that the Army uses on some of their exercises, well, we found a box of them and are stringing them up in trees, all they have to do is follow the little red and green glow. But again, we cannot sit there and wait while she is out here, hope you understand" Earl replied.

"Rocky One, you were told to stay put, but we will cover that later. For now, if you feel you must move on, please be advised that it is not safe to proceed. That is what we have professionals for. They are in transit. You should really return to the cabin" came the reply came.

"Roger, Susten Base, we understand, but for now, we must conserve our battery. It is important that we have radio remaining when we find Michelle. We will be off the air for about twenty minutes and call you again. Rocky One Out!" Earl concluded the conversation.

Moving the radio back to the channel with Michelle, Earl called to alert Michelle they are still on their way.

"Key your radio for me Michelle."

One burst of static returned.

"Michelle, Are you doing OK at this time? Earl asked.

Again, one single bit of static.

"Is your radio strong at this time?" Earl inquired.

Again one response.

"Michelle, the team is on the way, but maybe we can get to you first. We are still plodding through this stuff. Stay with us and do not go to sleep. We need to keep in touch with your radio. Do you read, Michelle?" Earl continued to question Michelle.

Again, there was that one response.

Continuing to proceed south, Earl and Joe, using flare for light, find the moving rough. There are many rocks that they do not remember, but they cannot follow a path.

After what seemed like hours but only a few minutes, Joe takes the radio from Earl, sharing the load.

"Earl, we will be in much trouble for being out here? But I would not want to stay in the cabin knowing that Michelle's out here alone. They would have to tie me to the main beam of the house to keep me back there. I know you feel the same way" Joe spoke to Earl.

"Joe, you bet we will be in some kind of trouble, if not from New York, from the Swiss National team that is coming. But we are making their job easier, all they have to do is follow the markings we are leaving" Earl replied.

Turning the radio on, Earl suddenly hears part of a conversation from Susten Base.

"Susten Base, We are on the air at this time. Was that last transmission for us?" Earl asked.

"Rocky, what is your distance from the cabin at this time? The rescue team wants to know. They are having a bit of trouble but are moving up and closing in on your location. They would really like it if you would return to the cabin, can or would you do that for them?" base asked.

"Base, we are about a quarter mile from the cabin if I can figure out this landscape. It is difficult to follow as it all looks different in this environment. We would like to continue if you don't mind" Earl replied.

"Rocky, if you are having difficulty knowing your location, be careful and return to base. You have already given us the location of Michelle, we can take it from here. The people that are in transit are really prepared to close in on the location you provided as soon as they arrive. They won't be at the cabin for only a few minutes to get their bearings. Please return to the cabin, they may be there before you arrive. They don't need three people to look for. There is a second team being prepared at this moment in case this thing takes longer than expected" Base responded.

"Base, we really want to continue, but I know the imminent danger we are in. We are not prepared to continue this search. We will return to the cabin, I would guess Michelle is about two miles ahead of our present location. That would take us until morning to get there. I hate to give up on her. She does not deserve this at all" Earl replied with a bit of sadness in his voice.

"Make it back to the cabin and wait for the rescue team. They will be there within the half hour if they keep moving as they are doing, they say the storm has let up a bit and they are able to make better time. Has the storm cleared any at your location?" Base asked.

"That's a negative at this time. The storm has not slowed down one bit. We are now in about 15 inches of snow and coming fast. I hope the rescue team gets here fast, Michelle will not like being left alone out here. She will be all over my case when we get her back to the cabin. I will try and call her to inform her that we are moving back and the team will be out and about soon" Earl said with a bit of sadness.

Changing channels again, Earl Calls, "Michelle, We have been in contact with Susten Base, they are demanding that we return to the cabin, neither Joe nor I are prepared to continue this trail, Base informs me that the rescue team will be on site within the half hour. Do you understand, one key please?"

There was soon one key on the radio.

Then another key.

"Michelle, I got the second key, what is it? Can you send me a Morse code on the radio? I will try and figure it out. It has been a long time since I used Morse" Earl replied.

Working with Joe, Earl listened closely to the coded message coming in from Michelle.

"Michelle, we understand your concern. We will not be out of touch with you. The team is bringing new batteries and we will talk to you. Our radio is in it's final stages. Stay close and low to the ground. The wind will not be so strong. I hate to have to return to the cabin, but you do understand, I hope" Earl stated with concern.

There was one last response on Earls radio. The gauge was showing near dead status of the battery.

"Joe, lets return to the cabin as quickly as possible, we will be able to follow the markers and it will be faster for us."

"Earl decided to try and reach base one last time." Susten Base, this is Rocky One, Do you read me?"

"Rocky, the team is now within a few minutes of your location, they will be looking for you. Please return" . . . the radio went dead.

"Well, Joe, I guess we are now on our own. I hope Michelle's radio stays up until they find her. We will return to the cabin and wait for them. They may be there now. God, I really hate to leave Michelle out there alone and not continue trying to find her. But those Swiss should find her without too much trouble" Earl informed Joe.

"Let's both of us take a flare and carry it high so the team can find us quickly. We will be easier to spot with that much light out here. This snow is really coming down" Joe suggested.

After walking back over the marked trail, following the red and green markings, they soon hear noises coming from the direction of the cabin.

"Earl, did you hear that sound? They are at the cabin" Joe stated.

"Let's get back as quickly as possible."

"Joe, I don't know if I can actually go any faster, I feel as though I have suddenly lost all strength to go any further" Earl countered.

Earl shouts to Joe. "I cannot get my legs to move through the trail you are breaking for me. I feel as though my legs are no longer with me. Maybe you can go on ahead and bring the team back for me also. One or two of them should be able to get me back to the cabin."

Joe stopped in his tracks and turned towards Earl. "What do you mean you can't move any further? What seems to be the problem. Are you feeling frostbite or any of the freezing signs?" Joe asked.

"Where does it seem to be the worst for you? I don't want to leave you here alone. One out there is enough. I will help you or I will carry you as far as I can. But I will not leave you here, do you understand?" Joe shouted.

Soon there were shouts being heard from the rescue team.

Joe let out a real scream so that they would be sure to hear him.

"Follow the red and green markers, we have a man down and need help fast!" Joe yelled back.

Within a couple of minutes the rescue team arrived on the scene with Joe and Earl. Questioning them, the team prepares a stretcher for Earl and start moving him back towards the cabin. Several men continue the trail with the markers towards Michelle's suspected location.

The team commander quickly put out the word that they had rescued one member and were now proceeding to look for the second. They had Michelle's location marked on a small map and figured it to be about three miles from the cabin. It would be rough going once they passed the mile point. The trail would then have many boulders and crevasses to cross.

With the sensing device they started to follow what seemed to be a different course then what Earl and Joe marked.

"Why are they going in that direction?" Earl asked.

"The radio signal indicates that she should be found in that direction" replied one of the medics on the rescue team. "It appears you were following an echo on the mountain. It happens frequently up here in the altitude. You were lucky you didn't go much further. It appears that there would be a rather steep drop not far from where you turned around. Our guys have already passed that point and determined by radio frequency that she is actually to the north. We have sent teams in both directions" the medic told Earl.

"Rescue One, this is Mountain Man One, We have a possible location on the victim. We have voice contact. She appears to be a bit incoherent but is talking. Will give you the coords on our next conversation. Tell the others to close in on my frequency. We may need lots of help, this snow is really getting deep back here" came a response after a long silence.

"Can we contact the base and tell them?" Joe asked the rescue coordinator.

"No, not at this time, we will contact them once we have a firm rescue on her. Once the team has her in their custody, they will contact us, we will then call our headquarters central. They will notify your headquarters. That is how we do it here in the mountains" the coordinator replied. "We do not want any false early report of this type of event getting out. We will let you talk in due time".

After another hour passed with very little conversation except for radio talk between rescue teams, there was suddenly a most welcomed transmission.

"Rescue One, this is Mountain Man One, Do you read"

"Mountain Man One, this Rescue one, yes I do read, what is your status Mountain Man?" The coordinator asked.

"Rescue One, We are having difficulty keeping her on the radio, we feel we are close to her, but she is not responding to our calls. We are circling our last locator indicator but are not getting any signals. Better get the other team up here to start in the morning" Mountain Man replied.

"Roger, Mountain Man, understand that you want me to call in the other team and have them standing by here, is that affirmative?" the coordinator asked of Mountain Man.

"That's affirmative, we are going to continue but we may need help by first light. It may take them a while to get to her. I wished we had asked them to start earlier. But get them on the way as soon as possible" Mountain Man responded.

Earl tried to get up from his bed, but fell quickly to the floor. Making enough noise to scare the coordinator who was studying a map of the area.

Joe and the medic quickly get to Earl and put him back in the bed.

"You are to stay there until morning. I do not want you attempting to move out of there unless you ask me first" the Swiss medic demanded.

"Rescue One, We have a fix on the girl. We have her on the screen. We figure that we will be there in about ten minutes. Do you copy?" Came a resounding call over the rescue man radio.

"Roger, Mountain Man, I copy about ten minutes to location of individual. Keep us informed as to what you find. We are waiting here at the cabin" the coordinator responded.

Moments later another call. "Rescue One, We have a rescue. We have a rescue, I repeat, we have a rescue, do you copy." The Mountain Man called in.

"Roger, Mountain Man, I copy, you have a rescue. Please advise of status as soon as you get a chance" Rescue One responded.

The coordinator then picked up another radio and started calling, "Swiss National Rescue Center, this is Susten Rescue Team, We have a rescue, repeat, we have a rescue, will advise of status as soon as Mountain Man confirms status. Do you copy?"

"Susten Rescue Team, We have a copy on your rescue, good job, hope all is well at your location. Please let us know status of individual as soon as you can. We will notify New York within the segment," a response came from the radio.

Joe could not contain himself, he hurried over to Earls bed and shook him awake. "Earl, they have found Michelle. They are not giving a status report as yet, but will soon. Isn't that great."

Soon there was another radio call, "Rescue One, We will need to stay here tonight, We do not want to move the individual, she is alive but moving very slowly. We are going to heat her up here. You can cancel the other team. We will have enough to transport her in the morning. We are going to spend the rest of the night here on the ledge. We have her wrapped now and taking measures to bring up the temps" Mountain Man stated.

At first light, Joe moves to the window of the cabin, looking in the direction in which he and Earl had headed, wondering how they could have made such a mistake.

Joe turned to the coordinator and asked, "Will she be all right? Will they start moving her down soon? Will it take long?"

"Young man, she is lucky to be alive, let's not rush getting her down from the mountain. We have asked for an air evacuation for both her and the young man. You will have to close up shop for a day and come down with us. We are waiting for the morning light to give the helicopter a safe flight. A second one is due in here about 0800 to get him. He may not realize it, but he was close to losing it last night, you two should never have gone out there like you did" the coordinator scolded Joe.

After a few days in the Swiss hospital, both Earl and Michelle were released and allowed to return to the mission. Both related the experience in different reflections.

Mr. Millo was quick to inform them both that they were to valuable to lose in such a silly manner. However, he clarified Michelle's case because she was on a project when the storm caught her. Earl, he had no excuse.

THE STORM

L ate in the afternoon, Michelle was minding the cabin while Joe went to town and Earl was out in the foothills. She looked towards the mountains and noticed the slowly developing clouds and gave them no thought.

Filing the last of the reports from the previous day, she walked outside and looked again towards the mountains. This time she noticed that the storm was closing fast and building as well.

"Better see if I can get a hold of Earl" she said to herself. "This storm is looking like it could be serious. I will call him and see where he is."

"Mountain Eagle, This is Mountain Princess, do you read?" Michelle spoke firmly. "Mountain Eagle, this is Mountain Princess, do you read?

Pausing for a moment she listened closely for a response.

"Mountain Cougar, This is Mountain Princess, do you read?" she tried Joe. Knowing he wasn't due back for several hours, she did not really expect an answer.

"Mountain Eagle, Mountain Eagle, this is Mountain Princess, do you read?" she called again. "Where could he be now that this storm is coming in faster than expected," she spoke out loud. It is not like Earl being out in this kind of storm. He knows these mountains better than anyone close to this location."

Turning the radio to a better radio station, she hears that there is a major storm blowing across the mountain valley. "Anyone in the Legend Range area should take immediate cover, stay clear of low areas and be aware of potential gully washers in the arroyos. Heavy rain in the low lands and heavy snow above 5000 feet elevation" the radio special announcement was broadcasting when she picked up a clear signal.

"That is our region, I wonder if Earl is close to here. But he doesn't answer his radio call. He probably is not aware of the seriousness of this storm" she spoke again to herself.

"Mountain Eagle, Mountain Eagle, this is Mountain Princess, do you read?" she called again.

"Mountain Princess, this is Mountain Eagle, I read you in a broken fashion, Mountain Princess, I read you," Earl responded.

"Mountain Eagle, there is a very serious storm brewing which you are more than aware of given your location", Michelle spoke, "Weather warning for the Legend Range, heavy rain and very heavy snow above 5000 feet, what is your present location?"

"Mountain Princess, I am about the 4500 foot level returning to camp. The weather is rain here, not to heavy yet but does look bad behind me" Earl spoke. "What are the winds to be, did they say" he asked.

"Mountain Eagle, the winds are to be very strong. That is making for a fast storm. Be sure you take cover and wait it out. We can get to you after the storm. That is if Joe gets back" she answered. "Keep in touch."

"Mountain Princess can you reach Mountain Cougar at this time?" Earl inquired.

"Negative on that Mountain Eagle, he is not due back for several hours yet. I expect him to return about four thirty" she responded.

"Mountain Princess, I suggest that you open the storm cellar access door in case you need to make for a fast break. The key is in the locker over the East window. Don't take any chances with a storm like this. They can be a real thriller out here" Earl spoke softly telling her to be prepared.

"Mountain Princess understands, open the storm cellar and be prepared. I am going now to do just that." Michelle responded.

As Earl turned to take another look at the storm he realized he would not be able to return to the cabin. The storm was starting to get very serious. "Better make for a cave in the next few minutes. There is no way I can make it to the cabin or to the next rest shelter. There is a small cave just ahead, I will hold up there."

Joe, shopping for supplies in town was not aware of the storm in the Legend Range area.

"That area in the valley is so beautiful" Joe told the store manager.

"Are you referring to the Legend Range valley?" the store manager asked.

"Yes, we are doing some research there" Joe answered.

"Are you aware of the major storm brewing out there? It seems to be real serious according to the radio on the last bulletin" said the store clerk.

"Are you telling me there is a big storm making its way across the valley?" Joe cut him off. "I better get out there quickly."

"I don't think it would be a good idea for you to start out that way now, to dangerous. Those valleys fill up quickly and swell over their banks with vengeance" the store manager said.

"I left an inexperienced research staff member in the cabin, She will not know what to do if the third member does not get back to the cabin in time. He is to be working in that area and the mountain foothills" Joe replied.

"Better try and call and inform them you are staying put for the time being" the store manager interjected. "I would not even attempt to go in that direction right now. You won't get ten miles before you are a serious statistic" he continued.

"Are you telling me I cannot make it to the valley at this time" Joe insisted. "Is that storm moving in that fast? I don't think I can reach the camp from here with the radio. We have no phone in the cabin. I can only try and get there. They don't know what I am doing, only getting some provisions. They are expecting me back before dark" Joe continued to make reasons for him to go over the road immediately.

"Young man, we don't have the staff in this town to be looking for lost bodies in the flooding arroyos just because you are being missed. You had better stay in town for a while. I don't know if the county has closed the road out there yet, but they will be doing so very soon" the manager continued to give reasons for Joe to stay in town for a while.

"What, they close the county roads for rain storms out here, what is that for" Joe asked.

"Well, to begin with, to keep people like you from becoming a fatality. We lose several people a year in this region due to them trying to outfox the storms that are brewing. If you listen to the radio after it passes, you will hear that we are looking for a hiker or two who were caught in the storm, either voluntarily or by not knowing the seriousness of the storm. Most of them think they can get into the storm and get some great photographs of it firsthand. The sad part is some of them float out instead of walkout" he filled Joe in on the details. "So you see, you had better plan on staying here. If your friends have a radio, call the station and have them broadcast it out to them. I hope they would understand your decision. Whatever you do, don't go around the barriers set up on the roads."

Joe, giving the conversation a lot of thought, turned and left the store. The sun was bright and the almost cloudless sky looked to good to be providing a serious storm anywhere close.

Securing the supplies in his vehicle, he thought about driving to the top of the ridge and take a closer look for himself. It would only take a few minutes to get to the ridge.

As he started to drive West, he could see several law enforcement cars and trucks headed West also. "I should get ahead of them, they probably won't let me go very far" he thought.

Noticing that the vehicles ahead of him were going into the local city hall parking lot, he started to think about getting ahead of them at that point. "Once I get ahead of them, they won't catch me and stop me" he thought. "I can at least get to the ridge and look towards the valley."

As Joe drove out the city limits he started thinking about what the store manager had told him. "Should I stop and turn around? I don't want to be a statistic in this way" Joe spoke to himself.

Turning on the radio in time to catch a bulletin, he listens intently, "If you are in the area between Legend Range and town, get to some strong shelter. The rains, coming out of the Legend Range is extremely heavy. Some flooding is already reported and expected to get much worse. Do not attempt to drive across the plateau or into the Legend Mountain area. It is very dangerous out there. Rain is about an inch an hour, winds about 50 miles per hours. Snow could be as much as a foot in the next three hours. This storm is unusual and not to be taken lightly." The radio report completed with other weather related items to the East.

Joe stopped his vehicle and decided to stay in town. Returning to the center of town, he went to the radio station to see if they could make an announcement for him.

As he entered the station, he could sense the urgency about the storm. Everyone seemed to be dedicated to doing something related to the storm monitoring process. As he walked up to the receptionist desk, he paused as he looked at the radar screen most people were watching. "May I help you?" the receptionist asked Joe.

"Hello Sir, can I help you mister?" she asked.

Suddenly, Joe realizes she is talking to him. "Yes, I need to see if you could make a radio announcement for me. I am part of a mountain research team, there are two people out at the base of the Range that are expecting me to return within an hour, I cannot get out there, obviously. Can you make an announcement to the effect that I will be staying in town."

"Certainly, I will call one of our producers and have them set it up with you" the receptionist told Joe.

As she called the producer, Joe continued to watch the radar screen. Amazed at the size of the storm, he knew nothing about the storm only a few hours earlier.

"Sir, you can go to stage three, they will help you there" she told Joe.

"Thank you for helping me" Joe replied.

As he walked back toward stage three, he could sense the urgency around the station. It almost seemed like everyone was fixed upon the storm. Approaching stage three, he is met by a tall straggly looking fella with a long beard. "Are you the fella who wants to get a message out to his research team" the tall guy asked.

"Yes," Joe replied. "They are expecting me within an hour, but I cannot get there obviously."

"Well, we are busy but I think we can get it in several times over the next thirty minutes. We have no way of confirming they can receive our transmission, with this type of storm. Those mountains do some strange things to our signals" the producer informs Joe.

"Whatever you can do for me" Joe replied.

"Just where are they located? Are they safe themselves? What names do they go by so we can identify them. Anything else you can tell us that we need to pass on to them?" the producer asked Joe.

"Well, the camp is in Legend Range, actually Legend Crevice is the location of the cabin we work out of. Michelle was to be there today. Earl was to be in the foothills today. We are known as Mountain Eagle, Mountain Princess and I am Mountain Cougar" Joe tells the producer.

"Well, what a bunch of names to work with. I wish you could tell me that the cabin was somewhere beside the Crevice" the producer stated.

"What do you mean by that?" Joe insisted on an answer.

"Well, this storm has reached that location, there are indications that the storm has stalled over that area, meaning that the rain may be as much as several inches an hour, that is very heavy. I hope the cabin is high and away from the arroyo. Let's get this message out so they may know that they don't have to worry about you at least. There is enough for them to worry about" the producer commented.

As he wrote notes to himself, he slips them to an announcer who is to broadcast it to the airwaves.

Feeling a little better about not trying to get out of town himself, Joe sets his thoughts to how the two will cope with this storm out in the range area.

Michelle, realizing the storm is getting very serious, opens the storm cellar door and moves papers into the cellar. Taking the radio with her she is caught up by an announcement that there ". . . is a Mountain Cougar who is caught up in town, cannot get back to a cabin in the Legend Range area because of potential high water. Also, that there is a Mountain Princess and Mountain Eagle out there in the Legend Range that should be advised that the Cougar will be OK in town. Cougar wishes he could be there also, but due to the storm, he will wait it out. If Mountain Princess and The Eagle can hear this announcement, please be advised that you are to take shelter immediately if you are not already there. This storm should be over the cabin you call home about now." The announcer reported.

"We wish you good luck and we will be looking for you immediately after the storm to check up on you. Please stay inside, this is a bad storm. Princess, the Cougar tells me you may be there alone, that the Eagle may be caught in the storm in the mountain. We hope he was able to get to your location before the storm came in. If he is in the mountains, he may be buried in snow shortly. Hope he is somewhere where there is good cover. Good Luck to both of you" the announcer stated. "We will repeat this again in several minutes to try and get to you.

Feeling relieved that at least Joe would be safe, Michelle could tell Earl.

"Mountain Eagle, this is Mountain Princess, do you read?" Michelle asked over the radio. "Mountain Eagle, Mountain Eagle, this is Mountain Princess, have just heard over the radio that Mountain Cougar is holding up in town. He had an announcement put out to let us know he could not get out of town. Mountain Eagle do you copy?" Michelle asked.

"Mountain Eagle, I am going to the shelter, very heavy rain and very strong winds here. Seems as though the cabin moves every time the winds hit it. Probably will be safer in the shelter" Michelle reported.

As she continues to move equipment into the shelter, she could sense the strong winds working on the outside of the cabin. Moving faster to get everything in the shelter, she knew she may only have a few minutes to accomplish the mission.

As she moved what seemed like the last piece into the shelter, the hand radio made a few sounds. Sitting the items down, grabbing the radio, she listens intently. "Who could be calling me over the radio? It has to be Earl. I must try and reach him again" Michelle continued to talk to herself.

"Mountain Eagle, this is Mountain Princess, do you read?" Michelle called. Static again. "Mountain Eagle, this is Mountain Princess, if you can hear me, this is the update, Mountain Cougar is holding up in town, heard over the radio station he is staying there. I have moved everything important into the shelter, the winds here are very strong, feels like the cabin is moving every time the winds blow. I wish I knew your status. I am currently in the shelter. Can you hear this transmission, key your mike several times to confirm" Michelle calls into the radio.

Michelle was not able to hear anything over the radio because of the ferocious winds blowing overhead. Soon she was able to hear some sounds like cracking lumber. Suddenly there was a loud crash and a lot of noise overhead. She stood frozen for a minute. "Sounds like the cabin just left me a pile of broken wood" she jokes to herself.

"Mountain Eagle, we just lost the cabin, I do believe it is now a pile of fire wood. I will check it out after the storm settles down a bit. Probably cannot get the door open now anyway" Michelle calls over the radio.

Working her way across the shelter in the dim light, she gets the feeling of being buried alive. There was a pile of lumber above her, hoping there was not a fire burning there also.

Again she hears the announcement from the town radio station confirming that Joe was not going to get out there today.

Preparing for a long night, Michelle moves several pieces of furniture around just to keep her mind active and not worrying about the seriousness of the situation. She knew she would be safe in the shelter.

Earl, sitting in the mouth of the cave, tried to communicate with Michelle. He could hear part of her conversation, but was breaking up. He was now sitting watching the snow accumulate at an unbelievable rate. "Never seen snow come down this fast. Must be six inches an hour rate. I better get back further into the cave. Hope nobody, especially a bear intends to use this area tonight. This is the kind of weather that makes them seek out this kind of cubby hole" Earl talked to himself.

As he moved further into the cave, he realizes that he is not alone. Taking his flashlight out of his back pack, shining it into the cave, he could see a pair of eyes looking at him. "Well, I guess we have to share this place together, I hope you don't mind. I will try not to disturb you too much, but we should really get further back into the cave. I know you can be comfortable near the opening, but I need to get back a bit further, it will be cold for me, do you mind?"

Moving further into the cave, he keeps an eye on the eyes that seem to be moving further also. "We won't go much further, friend, we are far enough for now."

"I must be able to see the opening of the cave, watch for bigger critters to come in. I am not expecting company tonight, but then I was not expecting to spend the night with you either. I guess things just worked out that way. I hope you don't mind my being here" Earl kept talking to the critter.

As the evening expired Earl pulled his light jacket from his backpack and put it on. The evening air was cold, damp even in the cave. The storm kept up its furry. He knew he was going to spend the night with some kind of critter. "Why don't you come out and identify yourself, critter" Earl insisted. "We are going to spend the night together, we might just as well get acquainted.

Suddenly Earl gets the feeling that he was being approached from deep within the cave. Turning around he could sense the critter moving towards him. He could make out movement but not the size or shape of the animal. This made Earl a bit nervous. The cave was not very tall at this point and he would have trouble making a fast escape if needed. The critter would certainly have the advantage in this situation.

Turning his flashlight on in the direction of the critter, he could see eyes getting closer. It was certainly too small to be a bear thank goodness. Could be a coyote. Whatever it was, it was moving towards him very slowly. Earl stayed very still, making moves very carefully so as not to disturb or spook the critter. If the critter wanted out of the night relationship, Earl was not going to stand in its way.

"All right, you can leave if you insist, just don't send for any friends, I am not available for your supper tonight. I will stay still and let you pass" Earl kept talking to the animal.

At the cabin, Michelle kept the radio on so she could keep informed of the status of the storm. She was fully aware of the potential flooding around her location. However, the cabin was high enough to be out of the flooding area.

Joe in the meantime, in town, was feeling a bit uneasy not knowing what was happening to his companions. Getting a hotel room for the night, he watches several reports from the weather people who indicate that the area of the range had been hit very hard with very high winds and torrential rains. Indications are that there may have been a possible tornado in the area of the Crevice. Joe sat up and got very nervous. He knew that Michelle was alone in the cabin, she was in the middle of that storm. Earl probably would have been locked up in the mountains somewhere.

Walking down to the local sheriff's office, Joe talks to the rangers assembled there.

"What do you make of the possible tornado in the area of the Crevice?" Joe asked. "I have several research partners in that area. I know that the girl is in the cabin and possibly the other fella, but most likely he was caught in the mountains by the storm" Joe informs them.

"Are you telling me that there are people out there in the old cabin near the Crevice Arroyo?" asked one of the men.

"Yes, we are doing a research project using that cabin as a headquarters" Joe replied. "We have been there for several days now."

"Let me inform the headquarters of this situation, we need to be ready to move as soon as the storm is over. If the winds are as strong as indicated, there may not be a cabin anymore. We have instruments in the mountains that are giving us very unfavorable information. There is very heavy snow in the foothills and torrential rain on the flats. That old cabin is in the middle of what we call extreme danger zone" the man replied to Joe and walked away.

Trying to get a conversation with another ranger, Joe realizes that he had set in motion some big wheels. That cabin had been monitored and reports were not good. No one seemed to have time to talk to him. There was a flurry of activity but all seemed to be going on behind closed doors.

Suddenly, "Hey Mister, come in here would you?" came an order.

Joe quickly went to the sheriff's office where he was met by several uniformed individuals.

"Gee, I hope we didn't violate any local laws by using the cabin in the Crevice. Our headquarters was to have it cleared several weeks ago" Joe said as he enters the building.

"No, you haven't violated any laws, but you did give us a bit of information that has us very concerned. Our instrument we have on the building has quit functioning. About twenty minutes ago in fact. Let us get some information from you, you can also call your headquarters, inform them of the possibilities of the situation. They must know as soon as possible that we may have several fatalities" one very distinguished man told Joe.

"Are you telling me that the cabin may have collapsed?" Joe asked very concerned. "How soon do you plan to get out there to check it out? Can I go with you when you go?" Joe was suddenly full of questions.

"Well, as soon as the storm passes over this area, we will be out in the chopper. We will have one standing by at the airport. We do not know if it will be possible for you to go along, better stay here. Tell us about the possibility of the other member being stranded in the mountains. How much does he know about survival? Is it possible he could have held up in some cave in the foothills?" The senior ranger asked Joe.

"Well, he is fully aware of the caves in the foothills, very smart about survival, he is our instructor on the subject. He was to be in the foothills directly west of the cabin. About the 5000 to 5200 foot range. He probably did not take along cold weather gear as we were not expecting any storm today" Joe continued to tell about the possibilities of how Earl would survive.

"Well, the storm is due over our location in an hour, we will have a chopper standing by, better yet, we will have one come in and take us to a point North of the cabin, we will move in when it is safe. That way we will be on the spot as soon as possible. The storm will probably lose a lot of intensity before getting here. It won't even seem like the same storm" the ranger told Joe.

As the ranger turned to walk away, Joe again pleaded to go along but to no avail. "We will have enough to take care of without taking you along, we know the area very well, we will find them for you" the ranger insisted. "You go and call your headquarters, now."

As Joe left the Sheriff's office, he could get a sense of security knowing that the rangers would be on the scene as soon as the storm broke. He continued to be a bit worried that Michelle was in the cabin when the last signal was received.

Returning to the hotel, he found a message waiting at the front desk "Are you from the mountain research team?" asked the clerk. "We have a message from your headquarters to call immediately. We were not sure if you were still in town or had departed with the rangers. But this call came in several minutes ago. I guess news travels fast when you are out in this part of the country."

As the storm started to let up over the Crevice Arroyo, Michelle made herself comfortable. Listening to the radio and the winds. She could tell the winds were letting up, there was less noise from the pile of lumber above her.

Soon she heard an announcement over the radio that there was a rescue team heading her way.

Jumping off the pile of boxes she had made a temporary bed, she turned up the volume on her radio in case they were trying to reach her. After what seemed all night, she heard a crackle on her radio. "Mountain Princess, do you read this radio?" came a call.

"You bet I hear your call, I been waiting for you folks. This is Mountain Princess, the cabin has apparently collapsed over me. I am in the shelter, below that pile of firewood. Have you heard from the Mountain Eagle. He is out in the storm someplace. I am OK for now, see if you can find him" Michelle responded.

"Mountain Princess, one step at a time, we know where you are, we have to find The Eagle. He is probably sleeping with a bear in one of those caves and is safe, we will look for him in the morning. Too dangerous to go into the mountains tonight. There must be at least 18 inches of new snow at his location. We are about twenty minutes from your location, we will call back and tell the Cougar you are safe. We will have you out of there with in the hour Princess."

The ranger team called back to town and informed Joe that Michelle was safe in the collapsed building. She had moved into the shelter before the building collapsed.

"Princes, are you hurt in any way? We will be using chain saws to cut you out, stay away from the area of the entry door. You are not going to be in any danger, the building shelter will not collapse any further" came a call on the radio.

Listening to both radios, Michelle was alerted by the big radio stating that she was OK and that she would be free within the hour. Michelle felt a few shivers go up her spine, knowing that so much attention was focused on her. She had not had so much attention since her kidnapping on the Atolls.

Shortly, there was a sound of some commotion above her. She could hear people calling commands, lumber being moved. "Princess, we are over your location, looking at what is here, I sure am glad you moved into the shelter before the storm hit. This place is a real mess here. Give us several minutes and you will see the outside world again. We will have a temporary shelter for our team set up here, and fly you back to town tonight. We will be out at first light for the Eagle.

Michelle now could hear the sounds of chain saws cutting their way through the wood pile. "Hey, you folks upstairs" don't mess up the office. We still have several days work to do here" Michelle called to the rangers above.

"Princess, we will do what we can to save your office. It looks like a mess now, but I am sure you will have it operational again in a few days" came a reply.

Finally Michelle could see the saw blades cutting through the door to the shelter.

"Looks good just to see the saw blades, gentlemen. What is taking you so long to rescue a women" Michelle asked.

As the wood fell into the shelter, Michelle received the first man through the door with a big hug. "You people are a real life saver" she commented.

Taking her outside, they took her to a tent. Several medical personnel asked their usual questions and then declared her fit to travel.

"Can't I stay and wait for Earl. He is still out there some place. I could not get an answer from him over the radio. I don't even know if he is safe. You people tell me he may be sleeping with a bear. What if the bear wakes up before Earl and is a bit hungry" Michelle jokes.

"We will get him in the morning. For now, you need to get into town, take a bit of time to recollect your thoughts. The chopper is waiting. One of our medical staff will accompany you to town. Joe is very anxious for you to return. He has your room ready for you. We will finish our reports with you in the morning, about 10 or so" the senior ranger insisted.

As dawn broke, Earl woke to feel something beside him. Slowly he turned toward whatever was there, it jumped, scaring Earl. As the critter receded into the cave, Earl could not identify it.

Moving towards the opening, He could see a very large pile of snow blocking the doorway. As he started to dig his way through the snow, soon he was able to see light.

Turning on his radio, he called, "Mountain Princess, this is Mountain Eagle, can you read this transmission?"

Surprised by the response, Earl moved outside the cave.

"Mountain Eagle, we were afraid you may have spent the night with a bear who may have woke up early and hungry. We have been trying to find your location. You must have been back inside the cave a ways" came a response.

"I don't know who you folks are, but it is good to hear your voices. What has happened to the world in the last twelve hours, I have been out of touch" Earl replied.

"We will fill you in when we arrive in a minute, we are almost to your location, a chopper will be there in two minutes, we have moved Michelle to town, she is OK, the cabin collapsed, but she was already in the shelter. If you want, and are able, you can head East about three hundred yards to the large open field, that is where the chopper will be able to land and take you out of there. We can see you now, what a sight. Are you dressed to walk through this much snow. We can bring in some snow shoes if you need them" the ranger stated.

"I don't have walking shoes for this kind of snow, can you bring in some?" Earl asked.

Soon Earl was aboard the chopper and on his way into town for a very cheerful reunion with Joe and Michelle.

A quick phone call to Mr. Millo to confirm all were safe and waiting to get back to work.

AIRCO 49ER

As the sun started to rise over the eastern mountains the alarms started to go off. Earl was first to come to the front door to see what kind of day was to be ahead of them. Soon Joe came out and stumbled across the living room floor followed shortly by Michelle from her room.

As the three stood in the open door, they could not help but look at the majestic splendor of the mountains to their west with the early sun bathing them. The snowcapped peaks seemed to be beckoning them to come on over. A fresh snow cover was apparent on the mountains. In a few more days and there would be snow in the meadow where their cabin was located.

As Joe turned around to start across the living room Michelle asked "Is it always this beautiful in the mountains?"

"Michelle, this is about as beautiful as it gets. There is such a peaceful atmosphere up here that you sometimes have to wonder why or how can things be so screwed up down on earth" Earl answered.

"Michelle, even though this is a real working assignment, the benefits of the beauty is worth every day of this assignment," Joe confirmed. "It would even be a blessing to be snowed in here for an extra day or two just because."

After breakfast, they sit and discuss how the day was going to be conducted. Who was going to do what and when it was going to be done.

"Earl, if you don't mind, why don't you take Michelle over to Wonder Valley while I go up to the top?" Joe made his simple statement and turned toward the door.

"Joe, you may need help up there" Earl countered.

"No, I am a big boy, I can handle this one day by myself, I've done it before. You take her to the Valley so she can see what is in store for us over the next couple of weeks. I can take her up to the top later." Joe countered.

"Hey you guys, don't fight over me, I didn't come up here to be fought over you know !" Michelle injected.

"No Michelle, we are not fighting over you, we just want you to get the best lessons possible, the best one here is in the Valley area" Joe remarked.

"All right, why don't we go to the Valley so I can start learning. I want to see what it is that makes you fellas always want to come up here" Michelle insisted.

"Keep in touch with the radio on Blinker One, Joe," Earl informed Joe.

As the three started out the cabin, there was a small twinkle of light from the Western mountains that seemed to say, "have a good day people, but do come and see us."

Walking out across the small meadow they soon reach the split in the trail. Joe takes the trail that will wind around several mountain valleys and up into the top range of the mountain behind the cabin.

Earl and Michelle take the trail that is relatively flat for the first several miles and then up a bit into the forested plateau to Wonder Valley.

Waving as they go out of sight of each other, they plan to meet again about noon on Schwartzwald Point.

Knowing he may run into some mountain goats, Joe was ready with his camera. Also, there would be snow ahead of him as he gained altitude. He walked slowly as to observe all sorts of birds and little critters getting ready for winter.

How they seem to know just when to start storing and how much to store, smart little fellas, he thought. He observes several woodpeckers that had not started down the hill for winter, no place for them up in the mountains in this kind of winter.

As Joe approached one of the many twisting turns in the trail ahead of him, he heard some sounds, like the goats he was looking for. He slows even more so as to not make any noise and scare of the goats. He rounds the turn and comes face to face with a herd of about twenty goats. They were on their way down the hill, meeting him face to face. Both bolted to the side of the trail. The goats scatter over the hill side, Joe just keeping a low profile for a while.

Figuring he could give them about ten minutes to regroup, he would just lay low and wait. As Joe was waiting, he could hear them working their way around the trail.

He knew he had blown his chance, but how was he to know that they would be using the trail. After all, they usually follow the rocky trail.

After his allotted ten minutes, he slowly got up from his hiding spot and moves toward the trail. As he methodically moves up to the trail and approaches the corner, he could see that there was still several goats standing on the trail. Great chance to get a few photos he thought.

Knelling slowly, he pulls his camera out and got a few great shots. Goats standing in every direction, position, on the rocks, over the bank, just everywhere. Well, he must get moving or be late for lunch at Schwartzwald Point. Couldn't even let that happen.

Meanwhile, Earl and Michelle were having a good discussion on the subjects of their research. They had about an hour to walk to reach Wonder Valley. "Better check in with Joe, he has a tendency to get distracted sometimes with his supplemental studies of wild life" Earl remarked.

"Blinker Two, Blinker Two, this is Blinker One, do you copy?" Earl spoke into the radio. "Blinker Two, this is Blinker One, do you copy?"

"Blinker One, this is Blinker Two, I copy" Joe replied. "I am in the middle of finishing up a few shots of the mountain goats that met me on the trail. I am just beyond the first switch on the mountain trail. Is that what you wanted to know?"

"No, Blinker Two, I wanted to know if you were going to meet us for lunch at Schwartzwald Point. What did you think we were contacting you for, to break up a photo session" Earl returned with his bit of whit.

"Blinker One, you have good timing. only two minutes ago I was in a critical photo session with these critters. They were really posing for me, very good shots with this herd. Probably wouldn't get this chance again in ten years" Joe responded.

"OK Blinker Two, talk to you again in about a half hour, keep in touch if you need something." Earl closed the conversation.

As Earl and Michelle continued toward their destination they observe the amount of fresh snow on the opposite mountain ridge. "Is that all fresh snow up there?" Michelle asked.

"Yes and some of that can be dangerous if we get to close. Our trail to Wonder Point comes close to the slide area of that mountain" Earl spoke softly. "Let's hope it was a wet snow and therefore not much chance of it falling as the sun works on it. We don't need to get into one of those avalanches today. Fresh snow is always dangerous and you just cannot depend on it staying where it was put" Earl continued.

Suddenly Earl stopped and motioned for Michelle to move over to the side of the trail. As they took cover, they could hear sounds from above. "What do you suppose that is?" Michelle asked.

"Well. If I had to say, I would think an aircraft. But there is not supposed to be anything up here in this quadrant" Earl spoke seriously. "It must be well of course and maybe coming down. We will need to get a fix on it so we can follow it."

"Blinker Two, Blinker Two, do you hear an aircraft going overhead now?" Earl asked Joe on the radio.

"Blinker One, there is an aircraft circling out over the meadow, not supposed to be here. What do you recommend, retreating to the meadow?" Joe asked.

"Blinker Two, if you can, go a little higher to see where it may be headed, keep me informed" Earl ordered.

"We are going to retreat to the meadow and see if we can locate or follow it. Also, I am going to try and make radio contact."

As Earl changed channel on his radio for attempted contact they turn and start back down the trail towards the meadow. "Unidentified aircraft over Hollow Mountain, this is Blinker One, what is your status?"

"Aircraft over Hollow Mountain, what is your status and where are you heading?" Earl asked again.

"Whoever you are, where ever you are, we are in trouble, one engine out and the other is now faltering. This is AirCo 49er, we have six passengers, two crew and we need to set down, no place now to do that, what can you recommend, AirCo 49er out"

"AirCo 49er, there is a small plateau in the valley, how much length do you need of unobstructed landing stripe?" Earl responded.

"Michelle, take the other radio, call Joe and have him come to the meadow. We are going to need his help."

"Blinker Two, this is Blinker One," Michelle went on the air, "Blinker Two, this is Blinker One, do you read me?" Michelle called into the radio.

"Blinker One, this is Blinker Two, I read you, what's up? I hear the plane, but cannot see him" Joe responded.

"Blinker Two, Earl wants you to return to the meadow, we have a twin engine aircraft in the area, one engine out, the other faltering. It needs to set down soon. Do you have any suggestions?" Michelle asked.

"Blinker One, I am on my way, the only suggestion I have is if the plane can make it to the Maple Flats and is not to wide, he could attempt to land on the road bed there. It is an old abandoned highway, only two lanes wide however. It is the only point close in this mountain valley where they could attempt to land." Joe replied.

"AirCo 49er, there is an old abandoned highway about three miles to your south, it is narrow and a bit short, about 3500 feet usable surface" Earl informed the aircraft.

"Roger, I hear you say there is one about three miles south, we will attempt to reach it, we are losing altitude fast. We would appreciate it if you could attempt to get to our potential location to check up on us. We will attempt to stay in radio contact with you also. Do you have any contact with the outside world, we seemed to have lost our radio for the outside world. Surprised you could get us on this channel" An anxious reply came back.

"AirCo 49er, we have three radios, we will attempt to reach our base camp and get them on the scene as soon as possible," Earl informed them.

"Michelle, get Joe on the Radio, tell him to go to the cabin and get on the big radio to try and reach base camp. They can call in the air rescue people and have help there before we get to the sight. We have some rugged country to cover before we arrive at the road he is talking about." Earl told Michelle.

Michelle radioed Joe and informed him as to what Earl wanted him to do. Responding quickly Joe started to move rapidly down the hill trail. Knowing it will take him twenty minutes to get to the cabin. The aircraft will be down in only a few minutes.

Earl and Michelle headed toward the Maple Flats area. Keeping one radio tuned to the aircraft frequency. The other tuned to Joe's radio. Earl knows that if he took a shortcut over one ridge, even though it would be hard, it could save them about half an hour. Checking with Michelle, she indicates she is willing to go over the short cut to get there quicker.

"You folks on the ground, we are not going to make it to the flats, we can see them, but we are going to fall short into the trees, hope you can get here fast." Then the radio went dead. No response from Earl's calls.

"We better get there as quickly as we can, they are on the ground now and need help!" Earl exclaimed.

"Joe, this is Earl, did you hear any indication of the crash? How far are you from the cabin?" Earl asked Joe over the radio.

"Earl, I am about ten minutes from the cabin, I do see some smoke in that direction. I am going to get in as quickly as I can and take the cycle down toward the scene. Do you concur?" Joe asked.

"Anything we can do to get there, we need to move in a hurry, keep up the fast pace, let me know when you arrive at the cabin." Earl requested.

As Michelle and Earl kept moving down the hill toward the potential scene, they begin to see a small smoke cloud rising from the area of Maple Flats where the plane was to be.

As they round one of the sharp corners allowing them a brief view of the mountains across from them, Earl thought about trying the radio.

"This is Blinker one on emergency frequency 01, is there anyone out there that can hear this transmission?" Earl waited a moment. "Keep your radio on channel 01 Michelle, I am going to try channel 9,"

"This is Blinker One on channel 9er, is there anyone out there that can hear this transmission?" He repeated.

"Blinker One, Blinker One, this is Gopher Alpha, we read you loud and clear on channel 01, can you go back to that channel, we will try and communicate with you."

"Roger, Gopher Alpha, Will go back to channel Zero One." Earl replied quickly. Switching his radio back to channel 01 Earl called Gopher Alpha.

"Gopher Alpha, this is Blinker One, we are on Hollow mountain, are you familiar with the location?" Earl asked.

"Yes we are, Blinker One, what is the nature of your emergency? How can we help?" Gopher replies.

"Gopher Alpha did you receive a call or hear a call from an AirCo 49er, a twin engine aircraft indicating engine trouble? We have one down in the vicinity of Maple Flats. We are about two miles from that location, last transmission from them was that they would not be able to make it to the old road for a possible landing strip. Could you check out that area for us and call the local air traffic control and alert them of the situation? "Earl asked.

"Gopher will be over the location in three minutes, we know that area well, we are over the back side of the old Hollow Mountain now. What is your location, can you pin point it for us. We are a small chopper, but can make a pass to identify ourselves" Gopher comes back.

"If you are a helicopter, you could possibly set down in the area and get to the aircraft. We are too far out to be of any help immediately," Earl replied.

After what seems forever, they receive a radio call from Joe stating he was at the cabin. Had called in the potential crash and help would be on the way soon. However, a storm was brewing in the mountains and they were not sure that an aircraft could get into that area before nightfall. It may be morning before anyone outside the mountains could bring in help.

Earl then informed Joe "that a small helicopter should have been over the cabin, they are on channel 01, let them know what you are doing so they can coordinate any activity. They can keep us informed of the weather."

"Roger, Blinker One, I heard one pass over a few minutes ago, I saw the smoke from the scene, we really need to get there" Joe said with a serious sound in his voice.

"Joe, take the cycle and head down there, take blankets and water with you. Sounds like you may be there for a while!" Earl instructed Joe. "We are still twenty minutes from the cabin, we will be down as soon as we get in to the cabin. I will bring the sled and crawler down. But for now, don't wait for us to get there, the chopper will be waiting for you."

As Joe goes out to get the cycle, picking up his radio, Joe calls, "Helicopter, this is Blinker Two, at the cabin are you at the crash site at this time?"

"Blinker Two, we are on the ground on the old road, we are leaving the chopper to go to the scene, it appears to be about 500 feet from the road surface, did not see any signs of life when we went over it. Do you know how many passengers were on the aircraft?"

"I don't know how many were on board, but just get down there as fast as you can, they need help now. I am coming down on the cycle, I'll be there in about two minutes" Joe answers.

"Were you able to get a hold of traffic control," Joe asked.

"Yes, we notified them of the situation, Blinker Two" Gopher Alpha responded. "Blinker One, this is Gopher Alpha, we are at the scene now, It doesn't look good right now, they were less than a quarter mile from the old highway. We will be off the air for a while. Gopher Alpha out."

Earl and Michelle arrive at the cabin minutes after Joe departed with the motorcycle. Earl asked Michelle to go in and get on the big radio to communicate with anyone about the situation. "I'm gone" she said and was out of sight in no time.

"This is Blinker One One, a research team on west side of Hollow Mountain, we have an aircraft down about two miles from this location. Does anyone copy?" Michelle calls.

"Blinker One One, this is Rescue Four Four, just how do we find your location? We had a report earlier that there was an aircraft down in the vicinity of a Maple Flats. We show no Maple Flats on either side of Hollow Mountain. Can you give us a good coordinate. We are also encountering potential weather. Do you have any contact with potential survivors?, Rescue Four Four, Over."

"Negative on any reports at this time. We have a small helicopter in the area on the ground, checking out survivors and need for help. They are going by Gopher Alpha. I don't believe they are in the bird now. We also have one of our team member on his way now on a cycle, he should be there now, barring weather problems." Michelle responded.

"Roger, Blinker One One, What is the closest marker you can tell us so we can get a location?" Rescue Four Four asked.

"Rescue Four Four, are you familiar with Wonder Valley or Schwartzwald Point?" She asked.

"Yes, We have a Wonder Valley on our map, Keep talking, we are beginning to get a fix on your radio location, We are North of your location, are there any features we should look for?" Rescue Four Four responded.

"Rescue Four Four, they say there is smoke coming from the crash scene, you should be able to see that soon, We are two miles west of Wonder Point, the aircraft is one mile southwest from our cabin. Can you locate that approximate coordinate?" she asked.

"Blinker One One, we now have smoke and a visual on your cabin, we are there in less than one minute, stay there, we will pick you up and go in together. How many of you are there at the cabin?" 4-4 stated.

"There are two of us here, but you can be better served if you go straight down to the scene, we have a cat to come down on?" she informed them.

"Roger, we are over your location in a moment, you can probably hear us now" Four Four stated again.

As Earl starts the Cat, he steps out of the shed to see the helicopter go over his head, flying low.

"Great, they were able to get in to check on them." He runs into the house to confirm that Michelle could tell him good news.

"Earl they are going straight in, not stopping for us, I told them to pass us up. They have no communication with Gopher Alpha. Joe has not checked in yet. Wonder what is keeping him?" Michelle said with a bit of puzzlement.

"Let's get out of here, have you called our base yet?" Earl questioned.

"No" Replied Michelle.

"We will get to them later," Earl stated "let's get out of here, someone needs our help. The cat should be warmed up by now and ready."

They leave the cabin and head for the cat, boarding, they are in motion soon.

"See if you can get a hold of either of the choppers or Joe, Someone should have a report by now. We know that Joe has a radio on him, try him first." Earl commented. "Blinker Two, Blinker Two, this is Blinker One, do you read?" Michelle calls in the radio.

"Blinker One, this is Blinker Two, I need your help, I have lost the bike and need help at the last point before Maple Flats do you copy, need help at the last point before Maple Flats." Joe returns the message.

"Blinker Two, understand you are down and need help, what is the nature of your injuries? We have just left the cabin in the cat, it will be several minutes before we can get to your location. Hang in there we are on the way." Michelle responded to Joe's call.

"Blinker One, I think I have just hurt my pride more than anything, but I am over a bank and just hanging on a tree waiting for help." Joe called back.

As Earl approached the location where Joe should have been, they slow the cat down to take a better look. He did indicate that he was over a bank hanging on a limb.

"There are skid marks there ahead of us!" Michelle yelled. "I can see them leading over the bank there."

Bringing the cat to a halt, Earl jumped out with a rope over his shoulder. Michelle follows him with a medical kit. "Joe, where are you?" Earl yelled.

"Joe, Where are you?" Michelle calls.

"Over here, the tree is getting tired of sharing my weight, hurry up and get a rope to me, before it lets me go!" Joe shouted.

Earl ties his rope securely to the cat and drops the rope over the bank to Joe. Joe securely ties himself to the rope and asked to be pulled up, his arms were sore from hanging.

As they pull Joe up the bank, he was greatly relieved just to be on solid ground, but wanted to get to the sight of the aircraft as soon as possible. He demanded to get into the cat and the three could go down together, Michelle could look him over while they were going down the last quarter mile.

Arriving at the scene of the aircraft, they meet one of the pilots of Gopher Alpha. "How are the people in the plane?" Joe asked

"Well, thanks to your fast action, help and following through, there are several survivors" We are going to try and help Rescue Four Four get them loaded and out of here tonight. We may need to place the deceased in your cat and have you transport them to the cabin." The crewman said.

"Which one of you is Blinker One? We need some additional information" said the pilot from Rescue Four Four.

Earl came forward to give them what information he could. As they finished the routine questions, he was asked if he would mind moving the bodies up to his cabin.

"No, we would be glad to move them up the hill, but do you think that is a good idea. Should they be left here or moved?" Earl questioned.

"If we leave them here, we will need to post a guard on them tonight. Don't want any animals getting into the remains. You know how that will be" the commander informs Earl.

"We must be moving the survivors out of here, you did a great job staying with the radio. We know how difficult it must be when you have to work several frequencies. We are getting out before that storm comes in on us," the pilot said.

Loading the survivors into the helicopter, they start it and are ready to move. As the helicopter lifts off, they signal that the storm is moving in faster than expected.

Earl picks up his radio and calls, "Rescue, if it looks too bad, stop at our cabin if you need. we have a lot of provisions there for prolonged emergencies. We also have a land line and long distance radio. Hope you make it out of the valley, don't take any chances" Earl insisted.

Turning his attention to the two in the other helicopter, he asked them to stop and check the weather before they leave the valley. Small aircraft and up or down drafts, do not make good company in storms.

After getting the bodies loaded in the cat, they start up the hill. Leaving the radio on so they could hear from either chopper.

Joe was a bit uncomfortable and bruised badly, but no broken bones.

"Blinker One, this is Gopher Alpha, we are going to sit down at your cabin and call in if you don't mind. How long will it take you to get to the cabin?" a call from Alpha came in over the radio.

"The door is not locked, let yourself in and make your call, please, in fact, please make a pot of coffee, I will need it by the time I get there" Earl answered.

"Thanks, Blinker One, we will, Gopher Alpha out." Alpha complies with the request.

As the cat approached the field where the cabin is located, they see the small chopper sitting out front. I wonder why they are still here?" Michelle wondered out loud.

"We will find out soon enough, Michelle" Earl replied.

Pulling up in front of the cabin, Earl shuts down the cat and approached the building. The pilot of the small chopper came out and informed Earl that there was a big storm coming in from the direction of the rescue helicopter flight plan. They may have to reroute the bird. Gopher wanted to stay close to remain informed. They had called their location in and were cleared for several hours if necessary, they could not get over to the back side of the mountain at this time.

Suddenly there was a call on the big radio in the cabin. Earl ran inside to get the call.

"Blinker One One, this is Rescue Four Four, we are going to go around the mountain passing your location again, don't panic, we will be back in a few minutes, more like fifteen."

"The storm is growing faster than we like. How much room did you say you had down there. We may need to spend the night if it is bad all around your location. We may need to call in the big rescue bird to handle this storm." Rescue 4-4 informs Earl.

"Rescue Four Four, you are certainly welcome here for the night, we have room and provisions, plenty of space to set down and some medical supplies here" Earl indicated.

Soon, the sky was filled with the sound of a helicopter returning to the cabin, Michelle and the pilot of Gopher Alpha go outside to look for the aircraft. "There it is," the pilot said. "It is coming in here, he must not be able to move around the mountain. Better make room for the night."

As the rescue helicopter approached the cabin, they pass once to pick a good location. On the second pass, they sit down far enough away from the small helicopter so as to not effect it.

Getting out of the helicopter, they inform Earl that there is a big helicopter coming in for the passengers, they just do not have enough size to fight the winds and storm. The big one will be on location within the hour.

"We need to move the injured into the cabin where it will be warm for them, make them comfortable and hopefully get some rest, do you mind?" the pilot asked.

Getting the injured into the cabin, Earl stoked the fire to increase the heat in the cabin and put on a pot of coffee and hot water.

The paramedic on the flight approached Joe and asked "How are you doing, I understand you went for a tumble yourself. Can I look you over to be sure that you do not have any broken bones? Maybe we need to put you on the big one when it comes in"

Joe agrees to be looked over, but states that he will not be loaded on the big one and hauled out. He was going to stay at the cabin.

After getting something to eat, all the crew members sit waiting for further information.

The waiting was soon over when the radio came to life. Rescue Four Four, Rescue Four Four, What is your location at this time?"

"Ah, the big one cometh," the pilot said. Taking the radio he responded with, "Big Rescue, this is Rescue Four Four, we are at Gro 66 and Pla 33. Our radio is on in the chopper, you can home in on it. Storm not bad here in this immediate location, visibility about three quarters a mile. Plenty of room to sit down and transfer passengers, What do you think your ETA will be," the pilot asked.

"Rescue Four Four, we are at Gro 33 at this time, it will be about a half hour if this storm does not get worse. If we have to go around the mountain, maybe an extra hour. How are the passengers doing at this time, any serious that must be moved immediately?" Big Rescue asked.

"None at this time, we have them all stable and resting, most asleep. The host here are really great people. They have made up coffee, food and warmed up the place for all of us" the small chopper pilot said.

In what seemed like a short half hour there was a sound of a big helicopter in the air. Earl and the pilot of Gopher Alpha go outside to watch for it. "I will spot him down over here on the flat, there will be a lot of wind, but it is better if we get him close to the cabin" the pilot informed Earl.

"Big Rescue, this is Rescue Four Four, We hear you coming, we have a place for you and are just waiting to get a visual on you." The pilot called.

"Rescue Four Four, our indicator says we are almost on top of your location, you have a real good beacon located in your chopper" came radio contact from Big Rescue.

"We have a visual on you," the pilot of Gopher Alpha stated, "you can come straight in and turn left on the pad as you sit down, I will set you down."

"Roger, Rescue Four, we have a visual on your location. We will be there in a moment."

As the big Air Force Rescue Helicopter sits down, three paramedics jump out and meet the pilot on the ground. The pilots of the big bird secure without shutting down the aircraft.

One of the pilots come out to see how things are with the passengers. The flight medic and nurse are already in the building, checking on the condition of the injured.

Getting them all loaded and asking for the deceased. They decide to take them also. Then off they fly into the snow storm.

They were airborne within 15 minutes. Indicating they could not stay any longer, they needed to get the injured back to the hospital.

Thanking the research team for their help and immediate response in saving the lives of several passengers in the plane.

The next morning the two smaller helicopters were able to lift off and faced into the sunlit mountain beckoning them welcome to the area.

Joe, demanding to stay, talked them into leaving him behind. As the three watched the small helicopters go over the mountain, they returned to the cabin and decided to get back to the research they were assigned to do.

SPRING

"Hey Earl look at these new signs" Joe calls out with excitement. Earl draws himself away from the desk and slowly moves outside where Joe was bubbling with all this new found excitement, "What is it that you have discovered?" Earl asked.

"Earl, look at all these new budding flowers, they have come out of nowhere! They weren't here yesterday. They must have popped out this morning" Joe exclaimed

"Joe, I love flowers, that is part of what makes this job so great, but for now, flowers will have to be put on hold. I really need to get these reports caught up before Mr. Millo calls for them. He should be here in a day or two to get them" Earl tried to explain away his lack of enthusiasm.

"Earl, I am going to go for a little walk and check on more signs of Spring. There must be more of them in the meadow. Maybe I should go up to the plateau and look" Joe talked on.

"Will Michelle be coming up with Mr. Millo?" Joe asked.

"She is supposed to bring along some new technology. She is going to that school now to learn new techniques to make our jobs easier. I don't know if she will be up or not. It will all depend on whether Mr. Millo wants her to try a sample of the new stuff. If she isn't coming up now, she will be up next week for sure" Earl confirmed.

As Joe turned to go up towards the meadow, he could see a bright lining on some clouds sitting over the mountain. "What a beautiful moment" he thought, "it must be a sign of great things."

Moving slowly up the trail, camera in hand, he is careful to observe everything he can. Taking many photos of budding flowers, trees and other subject matters he found along the way. "Earl should have come along, he could have finished those reports when we returned" Joe thought to himself.

"WOW!" Joe exclaimed as he reached the top of the hill and started across the plateau. "This is the world's most beautiful spot. Couldn't have picked a better spot if I had tried. If this plateau is so grand, what will the rest of the hollow be like in a day or two. I will have to bring Mr. Millo up here to see this. He will really be impressed. Probably want to step down as research director and return to field duty."

Slowing his already slow pace to just barely moving, he strolls across the length of the meadow. "It is a good thing I don't have to pay for the developing of film. I could take twice as many pictures at this point" Joe kept talking to himself.

As Earl finished the reports he stepped to the door and looked up towards the mountains. Picking up his radio, he calls Joe, "Flower One, where are you at this time?" Earl asked.

"This Flower One is in the middle of heaven on earth. I am at the far end of the meadow in a sea of flowers. This place is broken out with flowers, it is absolutely gorgeous up here. I am on my way to the hollow, want me to wait for you?" Joe asked.

"Yes, if you don't mind, we can walk and talk research at the same time. I am on my way up. By the way, I am bringing along some trail food, we will probably be out for a while, you seem to enjoy this kind of trail. I should be there in twenty minutes, will come straight up, not looking for any flowers or wild life" Earl stated.

As Earl starts up the trail, he is taken in by all the signs of spring. Flowers, new rabbits, buds on the trees and many other indicators. As he approaches the rim of the plateau, he spots several deer grazing.

"Joe, this is Earl, I am at the rim and holding for several deer in the middle. Have you gotten a fix on them. Look at the size of that buck!" Earl called.

"Earl, I have my camera on them, they have been in the meadow since you called. I have several shots of them, I would say that buck will have a number of points this fall" Joe replied.

"Have you seen any other signs of spring on your side of the meadow?" Earl asked.

"You bet, there are several porkys and a coon. All seem to be oblivious to my being here. When are you coming across the meadow?" Joe inquired.

"Joe, I am coming around, I am about half way now, I don't want to bother the master of the meadow and his lady" Earl responded.

"Well, you just take your time, this is splendor at it's best. It don't get any better" Joe called back to Earl.

"Give me a few minutes, I will be there. I have never seen this place so well lite up with such splendor. I thought you were a bit premature in coming up here. I have been here before in the spring, but this is the best floral arrangement I have seen here" Earl said with some real excitement in his voice.

"Earl, I can see you moving now, you have a few more minutes to my location. Find me if you can" Joe joked.

"Joe, if I don't see you when I pass your location, you will have to have a field dinner. I have your lunch remember" Earl came back.

"You won't get by my position, you can bet on that. I will be observing your every move" Joe responded.

Earl tries to keep his motion to a minimum so as to not disturb the deer and any other little critters in the area. Moving slowly, he keeps his attention to the meadow and brush around the plateau. As he watched all the many little critters, he was taken in by the activity of all of them. Stopping frequently to observe the sights.

"Earl, when do you plan to get here, today or tomorrow?" Joe asked. "I have been waiting for eternity for you to get my lunch to me."

"I thought I would spend the rest of the afternoon watching these little clowns moving around here. They seem to be oblivious of my being here" Earl answered Joe's question.

"Earl, if we don't move up the valley, we have twice as much work to do in the morning. We are already behind schedule. Will we have to do double duty tomorrow?" Joe questioned.

"Joe, don't worry about the work schedule, I just left the planning board, we are actually ahead of schedule for the week. It means we can watch nature bloom in this meadow as long as the sun stays up in the sky. We will have plenty of time" Earl answered again.

"Earl, stay where you are at for the moment, there is a bear moving in the West end of the meadow. She is trailing two cubs. I don't know your location at this time, but you are on an intercept course with them" Joe came back with a bit of excitement.

"Thanks Joe, I will make sure I stay clear of her. I really don't need to encounter them today. But will get into position where I can observe them for a while. Haven't seen cubs since last spring. I hope you are able to get a few good shots of them" Earl replied with interest.

Slowly, Earl moved ahead. He knew he certainly did not want to come face to face with the bear family. Moving so he could observe the West end of the meadow, he spots the mother bear, also noticing that she has caught the scent of something. She was looking toward his direction.

"I better get out of here, she must have picked up my scent in the wind. She may come to investigate quickly" Earl said to himself. Slowly he drifts back into the woods.

"Joe, I believe that she has my scent. Do you see her now?" Earl asked.

"Earl, you must have upset her peaceful lunch, she is headed towards the woods I believe you have occupied recently. You probably ought to get out of there as soon as possible, she is moving faster every time I look at her" Joe replied.

"Thanks Joe, I am going to pick up my pace and get out of here. Keep me informed of her where-a-bouts. If you lose track of her, you better come in my direction to assist me if needed. I know a hungry bear can do a lot of damage if not kept in check" Earl exclaimed.

"For now, Earl, she has stopped, the cubs did not follow her, she is moving back towards them, You are not going to be a bear dinner at this moment, so relax and enjoy your tour of the rest of the forest" Joe responded with his joke.

Earl decided that he would just keep up his pace and clear the area. He knew that the bear could change its mind and check out the scent it had caught earlier.

As Earl moved around the end of the meadow, he looked over so he could see the bear family. Looking further out, he could also see the deer still eating as if to not even notice the bear moving in the meadow.

"Joe, where are you now, I am just clear of hollow beech and coming into the small opening where you should be?" Earl asked.

"Earl, I can see you moving In the small trees, straight ahead. You probably have two minutes to my location" Joe came back.

As the two get together for lunch, they set down so they could watch the meadow.

"The Master of Art must have had a very good day when this was painted. This is absolute beauty. It does not get any better than this" Joe commented.

"Joe, there only a few assignments I insist on having. This is one of them for the Spring assignment. As you gain more experience, you will learn which ones to push for. There will come a time when you and I will be competing for the same assignments. You will already know which ones not to go for. If you take this one away from me, you are in trouble big time" Earl informed Joe.

Enjoying their lunch, they are interrupted by a call on the radio.

"Spring Lovers, where are you?" came a call.

"This is Spring Lovers, we are high in the worldly standings. We are at the meadow about a half mile above the cabin. Are you interested to come up and finish lunch with us?" Earl answered.

"Earl, I would like for you fellas to come down and get Michelle. She has been crying since you folks left her behind. I cannot understand why such a beautiful spot would interest her so much. Really, I would like for one of you to come down. I could send her up but would like to talk about some changes we need to make" Mr. Millo responded.

"Mr. Millo, we will be down in a about ten minutes. We want to get her into this assignment as soon as possible. She will really love this one. Tell her she can quit playing games now that she has her way. I thought you could handle her whining better than that. We will be there in a bit, but we do have to get around a family of bears" Joe came back.

Moving around the meadow, the two move down the trail towards the cabin. Keeping an eye at first on the meadow to not disturb the female bear.

As they return to the cabin, they enter to meet Michelle at the door and Mr. Millo sitting at the table.

"Hey you guys, what took you so long? I have been waiting to get a tour of the area." Michelle quipped immediately. "Where did you leave the bear you were complaining about?"

"She and the babies are still in the meadow, I hope she stays there" Earl said.

"Hello, Mr. Millo, it is good to see you in the field again. I know you don't get to see this kind of glorious beauty anymore. Would you like to go to the meadow or just over the hill?" Earl asked Mr. Millo.

"We have been looking at it all the way up the mountain road. This is without a doubt, one of the best spring assignments anyone could get. Michelle, you are definitely going to like this next several weeks" Mr. Millo answered.

Encouraging Mr. Millo to take a walk over to the meadow was the easiest assignment for Earl. He already knew that Mr. Millo enjoyed the Spring assignments in the mountains.

As they all left the mountain cabin for the meadow, they could hear some real loud barking and other sounds coming from up the trail. "Joe, bring the noise maker, it sounds like the dogs are out again. Better be prepared for this one," Earl spoke to Joe.

Indicating that there may be a little excitement on the trail, Earl informs Mr. Millo and Michelle, "You had better be prepared to see some things that are not going to look pleasant, but we will have no control over them."

As the three move up the hill rather slowly to prevent making a lot of noise, they could hear the noises getting louder.

"Mr Millo and Michelle, we are going to have to go off the trail for a while, those are probably wild dogs and we don't want them to get our scent. Joe will know where we are. I will call him and tell him we are leaving the trail. He will understand" Earl told the two.

"Flower One, This is Earl, we are leaving the trail at Box Junction to avoid scent trails, do you copy?" Earl asked Joe.

"Roger, I copy, will call when I get close to the Junction. I will also bring the rifle, just in case" Joe responded.

"Good idea, make sure that you bring the repeater, sounds like maybe ten or more from this point".

"They must have something trapped in the hollow, please come us as soon as you can."

"Earl, I am leaving the cabin at this moment. Will be there in about ten. Cannot run up the hill like I used to do. Motor must be slowing down. But will be there soon, will call you from the junction, unless you call me earlier" Joe answered.

Hustling up the hill side, the trail soon brought into sight the Box Junction. Joe called Earl, "Earl, this is Flower One, I am at the Junction, what should I do, which way should I proceed please inform?"

"Joe, take the tracker trail, it will get you here quickest. We are watching the bloodiest battle of the Spring, please come up as quickly as possible." Earl spoke softly.

As Michelle watched the battle going on just below them, she was moved by the amount of stamina involved in the critters doing battle. "How long can this type of battle go on?" she asked.

"Well, if it was allowed to continue till death, it may last another five minutes at most. If Joe gets here quick enough, we will have a sick critter on our hands but not a dead one. But that is the nature of Mother Nature to feed her own" Earl responded.

Mr. Millo spoke softly, "what are you going to do with the rifle, shoot one and watch the rest run off?"

"No, the rifle is for our protection. If the winds change and they notice us here, we are their next victims. They will attack us instead of the other critters. I don't feel like being a dinner for any one of them ugly critters" Earl said.

"Earl, I am almost there, I can see you in the brush over the pit. Where should I enter your zone?" Joe asked.

"Joe, just come straight to our point. I don't trust the winds here. There are to many of those dogs to fight off without your weapons. We have already selected our trees to climb if they catch us here watching them. I don't believe it is worth saving the critter with the fighting he has already done. Mother Nature will have to take care of this one" Earl joked.

Arriving at the meeting point, they all watch the remaining fight. Not much fight left in the critter at this point.

Suddenly there was a crashing sound behind.

As they all turned around, they were almost face to face with a large female bear with her cubs. She was intent on getting a human dinner for her own self.

"Joe, you have the rifle, you stay behind and let us move out smartly, but intelligently" Earl instructed. "You do what you have to do, but try not to shoot her if you can help it. We will be moving West."

"Yea, you folks move off West, I will take her South, hope I can stay ahead of her. After I start moving, one of you move in the direction of her cubs, she will be distracted and take that route. I will then get a little breathing room. Let's move out of here fast" Joe commented quickly.

Earl lead Mr. Millo and Michelle West for several steps, motioned for them to keep moving, he turned to intercept the cubs for a moment.

"Keep an eye on the dogs down the hill, if they start moving in our direction, take a tree" Earl yelled. "They may want to come up and investigate the action."

Earl turned quickly to see what he could do to distract the huge black bear. As he turned, he noticed that the dogs were splitting in two groups, part of them were now on their way up the hill. Now, what a decision, he was heading in the direction of the cubs, the mother bear was after Joe, and the dogs were coming after all three of them. "Not a good situation," Earl thought.

"Mr. Millo, you and Michelle, take a tree fast, the dogs are coming. I must get a trail broken for Joe and get that bear off his tail. We are into a victim versus victim situation at this time. I must get to Joe" Earl called again.

Looking over the short range of woods ahead of him, he could see Joe moving ahead of the bear. She was not very aggressive, she was moving about the same pace Joe was moving.

Suddenly, the mother bear realized her cubs were also in danger, spinning around and moving fast towards Earl's position. "Joe, she has turned, please be aware that the dogs are also coming, I may need to have you take one or two out. I am trapped between the oncoming dogs and the bear. Please come to my aid, Now!" Earl shouted.

Earl took to climbing a small but straight tree. He knew that the bear would have trouble climbing it but would be able to shake it very vigorously if she wanted to. Moving up to about the 15 foot level, he waited for the bear. As she arrived at his point, she was again distracted, this time by the dogs, who had caught scent of the cubs. The cubs would be a better meal than Earl.

As Mr. Millo and Michelle sat in the tree helplessly, they wondered how the fight over the hill was coming, there certainly was a lot of noise coming from that direction. Joe cautiously approached the ridge where he could get a glimpse of the action that started all this. To his amazement, there was several dead dogs laying on the ground, the critter they were attacking was standing all by itself but appeared to be watching something in the heavy brush.

Turning his attention again to Earl's situation, the bear was now involved in a standoff with three dogs.

"Earl, shall I take one of them out and that will scare off the rest of them?" Joe summoned Earl.

"How does the battle over the hill look? Sounds quiet now, where are the other dogs? What is going on down there?" Earl questioned.

"Earl, there is something strange going on down there. There are two or three dogs laying on the ground and something big in the brush, I cannot make it out. But the critter has survived and is looking into the big brush" Joe replied.

As the bear and dogs sparred, they were soon interrupted by the appearance of a large buck. Blood was staining his large rack. He had been in some kind of a fight himself. Swiftly, the buck charges the dogs, and hits one in the rear quarter with his great antlers. Swinging his head abruptly, the buck throws the dog from the fight. Moving quickly again he strikes the second one. The third dog soon gets the hint that he is fighting a losing battle.

With the dogs now running from the scene, the deer took a look at the huge black bear that was starting to settle down a bit. The buck snorted a large snort and looked at the bear gain. The mother bear turned and looked at her cubs, being all right, she looked back at the buck and growled.

The master of the buck herd looked slowly at the ridge, there was the critter, having only a few major cuts, but would survive. Turning his attention to Joe, the buck snorted twice, shook his large rack and turned around to see Mr. Millo and Michelle. Snorting again, he moved in their direction, stopped and looked up at Earl, shaking his head up and down as if to be beckoning Earl to come down.

Slowly Earl started to move down the tree. Keeping an eye on the bear because he knew she would not listen to any deer if there was any possibility of her cubs being in danger.

As the buck moved slowly to the tree where Mr. Millo and Michelle were staying, he repeated his motions. Turning again to face the bear, the buck walked slowly with his stained antlers held high.

Joe moved slowly towards the ridge and away from the bear family. Earl reached the ground and he also slowly moved in the same direction.

Mr. Millo and Michelle were not so quick to come down. When the buck returned to the tree, he snorted seriously and stared at them. Moving back away from the tree, he scuffed his front foot hard on the ground as if to say to them, 'come down this moment.'

Slowly they start moving, the big rack of antlers standing guard for them. As they reach the ground, the buck moved his head in the direction of where Joe and Earl was standing.

As the bear again started to move in their direction, the buck stood in front of her. He seemed to know that it was his responsibility to break up the fighting in the forest. The big hungry bear slowly turned and went back to cub tending.

"Earl, do you suppose that the buck took care of the dogs there in the valley and then came up to rescue us. He seemed to know where to make each move?" Joe asked.

"There is a good bet, that buck knew where he was needed. He has a few marks on him, but he stood his ground. Let's get out of here before he decides we are his next targets. Did you see the way he threw that one dog? Must have thrown it twenty feet" Earl said with excitement in his voice.

As the four of them looked with total astonishment, they move away from the hill ridge.

"Earl, what was the incentive for that buck to step in?" Michelle asked with a serious question.

"Michelle, this is Spring on the mountain. This is his hill. He knows what has to be done to maintain peace as best as possible. He certainly was a master of the situation today. Glad he was here to break it up. Dogs, bear, deer and critters, what an exciting moment for us all" Earl answered her questions.

"Mr. Millo, shall we continue up the range and take in the peaceful tranquility of this mountain?" Joe spoke to Mr. Millo.

"Joe, if I didn't know any better, I would think you were joking. But you are serious. Yes, I want to go on up the trail. This has been a real experience for me. In all the years I spent out here on mountains, I have never seen anything like this exhibition" Mr. Millo replied.

As the four move up the trail, they take one last look at the huge buck, standing between them and the mother bear. The buck, with his antlers held high, was seemingly moving his head up and down with approval. Standing there also was the critter that had been initially attacked by the dogs. It was close to the big buck but away from the bear.

Arriving at the upper plateau, they stop and take in the Spring carpet of flowers on the surface. "Michelle, will you be picking any of these flowers soon" Mr. Millo asked.

"No, No" she came back quickly, "It is so beautiful here I would not want to disturb anything. I just don't know about working in the hills with the bear around," she was quite upset today.

"Well, let's move around to the other side and take a good look at the best pad of this assignment" Earl interjected.

"Earl, does it get better than this" Michelle asked. "It looks like what I would picture as the ultimate beauty of the world here."

"Michelle, we have only just begun to see the majestic beauty of this valley. Wait until you get a look at the sight just minutes ahead of us if we don't run into any more dogs" Earl responded.

Moving around the hill, they come to the most perfect spot in the world. Flowers, snow and fresh water running peacefully of the mountain surface.

"OH, I love this, look at the snow, so pure, the water so cold, and yet the flowers are blooming as if to say, 'It is time to move on now'" Michelle came to life with excitement.

"Well, we had better start back to the cabin now" Joe spoke. "I hate to be the one to bring this expedition to an end, but we need about a half hour to get back to the cabin, will be getting cold here soon. Let's take the Sledge Trail, Earl"

"Good idea, it will be easier and probably less troublesome for other critters" Earl concurred.

"What is Sledge Trail" Michelle asked.

"It is the trail used many years ago by settlers to move lumber off the hill and also stone for building" Joe answered.

As they move down the trail, they were captured by the thought that they were being observed. Looking up on the ridge above them, there was a large rack moving slowly along. As they stopped to admire the huge rack, they could see the motion of the buck stop and then seen it looking over the ridge at them. "I do believe we are being told to keep moving" Earl instructed.

As they reach the cabin, there was a definite chill in the air. As Michelle turned to take one last look over the beautiful valley, she could see the 'master of the mountains' standing in the meadow, with him was a doe and a pair of fawns. "Look you guys, isn't that the epitome of nature? Standing proudly over his watch, he now can bring her out and let us see what he is so proud of" Michelle called.

As the four settle into the routine of discussing the events of the day and future encounters on the mountain, they hear a small commotion in the front of the building.

Earl slowly raised out of his seat to take a look. There in front of him was the huge black bear and cubs, she was looking in as if to apologize for her being aggressive on the mountain. Calling the others to the window, he could make out the outline of the big buck standing nearby.

"It must be our lucky day, we have witnessed a very strange set of happenings today. I do believe the master of the mountain must have informed the black bear to come down and say she was sorry, but that she was only doing her duty to protect her cubs" Earl stated.

"Let's finish this discussion in the morning, we have all had a very busy, exciting day. One we will all remember for a long time" Mr. Millo stated.

At first light, Earl was looking out the window at the fresh dusting of snow and the flowers breaking through. Fixing a pot of coffee, he slowly moves around the cabin, waiting for the time to go into the hills again.

After breakfast, they all bid farewell to Mr. Millo and watched as he drove down the mountain. Michelle turns and looks at the two men, "Well, what are we waiting for, we have work to do, the boss is not coming back for another three weeks".

Looking up towards the ridge, Earl can again see what appears to be a large shape, must be the protector, he thought.

SNOW ONE

As the snowmobile climbed into the fresh mountain snow, Joe, the operator, noticed the weather ahead looked questionable. Joe and Earl were on a mission to resupply a remote camp about three miles from base camp. Most of the trail would be up hill with several small downhill runs. Radio communication had not indicated any bad weather. They had left base camp early enough to get to the remote site before lunch.

The trail was rather steep in several places and very narrow in others. As they started the mountain trail, Joe was thinking of the possibility of turning back. Neither Joe nor Earl wanted to be out there in the snow and stranded on the mountainside. As they approached the point of no return, Joe stopped the machine to talk with Earl.

"What do you think about trying the mountain?" Joe asked.

"I think we had better turn around and go back to base. We can call them from there and let them know we are not coming", Earl said.

"I was thinking the same" Joe replied. "I would like to get the supplies up today and not have to worry about them tomorrow" Joe continued.

"Try and reach base from here and let them know we are returning" Earl instructed.

After several attempts to reach base, they knew the hill was blocking their radio signals. "I will stop down the hill in the big curve to try again," Joe commented.

"In the meantime, we had better get started down the hill."

As Joe turned the machine around, they sighted what appeared to be either smoke or fog coming from across the valley.

Earl was first to speak of it, "I don't believe we have anyone up in these mountains except our remote camp, do we?"

Joe was quick to concur with that. "Far too dangerous to have people out and about now" Joe replied.

As they started down the trail, they could see what appeared to be a fire burning on the opposite mountainside. Joe stopped the snowmobile for a better look and a chance to study the area. It certainly was a fire all right. How could a fire get started out there with that much snow on the ground.

"Earl, do you want to try and reach base camp again?" Joe asked. "Maybe we can reach the remote camp now."

Not being able to reach the base camp, and trying the remote camp, there was an answer. "Joe, I have someone on the radio, but it is not our camp. Turn the snowmobile off, I can barely hear them." Earl stated. "It does appear to be someone from another camp somewhere." As Earl tried to again get a response, he kept a close eye towards the valley where the smoke appeared to be coming from.

"This is Snow One" Earl called into his radio, "Do you hear me? This is Snow One, can anyone hear my call?"

"This is Rival Two, Where are you and what can we do for you? This is Rival Two, can you repeat your location and state your problem." came a response on the radio.

"Rival Two, this is Snow One, we are with the Mountain Research Group, at coordinates Zulu four with the state research group. We are attempting to locate the source of fire on the Echo Mountain, East side. Further, we are returning to our base camp, we cannot reach our remote site and must return to our base. We cannot raise either camp on our radio. What is your location?" Earl asked.

"Snow One, this is Rival Two, We are somewhere overhead. We are part of a small plane race. We are probably directly over you location now. But there appears to be a snow storm between us. We see no evidence of smoke but will look closer now. What is your status and how can we reach either camp for you? We will try and get an answer for you."

"Rival Two, You can try and reach Camp Zulu on CB channel 4, if that does not work, try and reach Zulu Camp Two on CB 4 or Emergency 5. We are attempting to return to base camp. Would like to take time to check the fire source and then return to base. Can you try and contact base camp and tell them, they need to get some type of equipment out to work on the fire. Thank you Rival Two."

Earl turned toward Joe with a puzzled look, "Why can't we hear the plane if they are overhead?" Joe looked at the sky and shook his shoulders at the question. Joe moved around to get into position to restart the snowmobile. "No," Earl stated, "let's wait for a moment to see if we get an answer from the aircraft."

"Snow One, Snow One, This is Rival Two, do you read?" came a response on the radio.

Earl scrambled to the radio, "Rival Two, this is Snow One, I read you loud and clear."

"Snow One, Snow One, This is Rival Two, how do you read this transmission?" came another call.

"Rival Two, I can read you loud and clear. I can hear you very well, Rival Two" Earl again responded.

After another silent minute, the air wave again came alive with the voice on the radio calling for Snow One to answer. Earl took is hand held CB and moved it to channel 4 and returned his call. Nothing came back from the radio, moving it to channel 5 for emergency broadcast, he still did not get an answer.

"Snow One, We are not able to get a response from you, but if you hear us, proceed to base camp. Action will be taken to check out the fire. Mountain camp has been informed that you will not be able to proceed upwards. They are aware you are returning to camp. This is Rival Two, we will attempt to stay with you until we hear from you or your base. There appears to be a breakdown in the communications systems. Please standby, we have another message coming in from your camp, will return in a moment, Rival Two out."

"Snow One, this is Rival Two, if you can hear me, your base camp advises that you move into a safe area for the night. There is a storm coming and they don't figure you can get out before it comes in. We are apparently not covering the same area, we are not experiencing any type of weather you are looking at. Please advise if you can hear me, Snow One, Please acknowledge if you hear me."

Earl keyed the microphone, sometimes that will work for a positive response. "This is Snow One, Rival Two, can you read the microphone."

A firm response came over the receiver, "Snow One, this is Rival Two, We do hear a mike key. Please respond again with a double so we know it is you". Earl grabbed the mike and again keyed it two times. "Snow One, That was your response, we are unable to communicate with you directly, but you can key your mike to respond. Did you hear the message of the incoming storm?" please give me two keys.

Earl keyed the mike twice and waited for the next question. "Snow One, Rival Two again, Can you find a place to stay for the duration of the storm?" Earl keyed the mike three times. "Snow One, We received three keys, does that mean you cannot find a place in your area for the night?" Please give me two for an affirmative and three for a negative."

"Snow One, Please hold, we have another message coming from your base camp."

With that, Joe and Earl started to looking for a better place to spend the evening. That would mean having to put up the storm shelter. They would have to go down the hill a ways and hope they would not be in line with the fire if the winds shifted.

Joe suggested that they go a ways while the weather was still looking good. But if they started the snowmobile, they would not be able to hear the radio call where was he calling from anyway. They still could not hear any airplane.

After what seemed like minutes, actually moments, the radio came to life again. "Snow One, This is Rival Two again, help is on the way, they have an Arctic Cat coming, will probably be on your location within two hours, can you hold that long?"

Earl keyed the mike twice. "Snow one, are you in any immediate danger of the fire?"

Earl keyed the mike three times. "Snow One, we are apparently not in the same valley, there is another radio coming in the area, maybe we can get a fix on your location, key you mike again, four this time."

Earl keyed his mike four times and waited.

"Snow One, from your base camp location, I must be about 20 miles from your location. I can see a storm in that direction, will attempt to get closer, but must stay away from the storm itself. Snow One, Are you currently moving?"

Earl keyed the mike three times.

"Snow One, are you able to move?"

Keying it two times, Earl was getting excited about moving down the hill.

"Snow One, will you be able to communicate if you are moving down the hill?"

Earl keyed three times.

"Snow One, is the weather bad there at your location at this time?"

Earl keyed the mike twice.

"Snow One, if you move down the hill, will your radio still be able to reach out and communicate, give me four if you think there is some question?"

Earl keyed the mike four times.

"Snow one, Stay there, I will again communicate with your base camp, if I can. I need to know your location. Please standby."

After a few minutes, Rival Two came back on the radio, "Snow one, I must get out of the area. I am beginning to loose lift and need to get back up in the air. There is another aircraft but he cannot hear your keying. He is probably to far out. Your base camp knows you approximate location and they do have a cat on the way. Sorry I cannot stay around to give you further assistance. Rival Two out."

Earl keyed the mike twice to let him know he appreciated the assistance.

Joe started the snowmobile and turned it toward the downhill trail. Earl came over and asked, "Do you think we can make the Rustlers Corner area before the storm comes in, there are plenty of trees there and they can protect us?"

Joe nodded his head and revved the engine as if to tell Earl to get on. Studying the weather, Earl slowly mounted the rear seat and they started down the trail. Earl kept the receiver close to his ear in case there was a message on one of the radios. He was hoping to hear from base camp.

Rustlers Corner was about a thirty minute drive from their present location. Going down would be easy if they don't run into weather. That would only slow them down, the trail would be fairly easy to follow even in a storm.

Earl kept trying to raise the base camp on the radio, but nothing came back to him.

Stopping now and then to check the location of the fire, they could see that the wind was pushing it away from their projected location, at least for the moment.

Earl, trying the radio every time they stopped. "Camp Zulu, this is Snow One, How do you read? Zulu two, this is Snow One, How do you read?

Nothing.

After a moment, Earl went on emergency radio, "This is Snow One, a snowmobile on East Echo Mountain, does anyone read this transmission."

"Snow One, this is Primrose One, we are on the west side of Echo Enchanted Mountain, we must be close to your location. We are located at the 8000 foot level on Woody Plateau. Are you familiar with the location? Do you read, Snow One?"

Earl quickly responded "Primrose One, This is Snow One, Yes I do read and I am familiar with the location. We are about two miles South of that point. We are weathered in and cannot reach our base camp, Camp Zulu on channel four. We are going to stay in the area of Rustlers Corner tonight. Can you attempt to reach either Camp Zulu or Zulu Two on channel four and let them know we are stopped for the night? Or at least we will be in ten minutes when we reach The Rustlers."

"Snow One, this is Primrose One, We will attempt to contact one or the other, please stand by your present location until you hear from me. Primrose One out."

"Roger that Primrose One, but we would like to reach Rustlers Corner as soon as possible, we have a fast developing storm coming straight at us. We will move down to the Rustlers and stop for the night and await your call."

"Snow One, if you do move down into the valley further, I may not be able to raise you on the radio. I am having trouble hearing you now. Please stay put until I can respond to your request."

"Roger, Primrose One, wIll stay put for ten minutes." Earl stated.

Knowing that they had reached another radio made both men feel more comfortable. Why can't they reach base camp, they have not had this problem before.

After what seemed like hours, the radio again came to life.

"Snow One, Snow One, this is Primrose One, How do you read?"

"Primrose One, This is Snow One, I read you loud and clear." Earl called back.

"Snow One, Snow One, we are unable to reach either camp you requested, proceed down to your overnight spot, we will attempt to reach you there in fifteen minutes. Do you read, Snow One?"

"Primrose One, We read loud and clear, proceed to overnight spot, Rustlers Corner. Will attempt to contact you when we arrive at Rustlers Corner. Please confirm your receipt of this message, Primrose One."

"Snow One, you will attempt to contact us when you arrive at Rustlers Corner, Primrose One out" came a response.

Joe started the machine again and they continued down the hill again, "Hope this snow doesn't get any worse," Joe stated.

"We may have trouble getting to the corner. Where did this storm come from, other than from the valley and we did not hear base calling to alert us. We now must be alert for the storm and the winds, in case of a shift, the fire. One of us will have to stand watch tonight." Earl stated.

After a couple minutes heading down the trail, Joe could see the snow starting to accumulate faster than he liked. It was really piling up fast. Only five more minutes, he thought. Any further delays and they might have trouble setting up camp

Not soon enough Rustlers Corner came into view, they had a hard time locating the drive off to where they could park the snowmobile. Almost six inches of new snow, hard to believe that much in such a short time. Joe parked the machine close to the base of a large evergreen tree.

Looking around for another tree, he decided to pitch camp next to the snow machine. The tent they had could be set up next to the snowmobile so as to draw heat from the engine if necessary. That would save on having to keep a fire burning all night, just having to run the machine every hour for a few minutes.

Earl took the radio and walked out into the open away from the camp, "Primrose One, this is Snow One, Primrose One, this is Snow One, Do you read?" "Primrose One, Primrose One, this is Snow One, do you read?" There was no response.

"Zulu One, this is Snow One, do you read? Zulu Two, do you read? Arctic Cat, do you read?" Earl repeated.

"Does anyone read this transmission?" Earl was getting a bit nervous. If the Arctic cat was still on the way, they would be picked up in an hour or so, but better set up camp just in case.

The camp was set close enough to the trail that if the Arctic cat did come along, they would have time to get to the trail before it passed their position, besides, they were informed that Rustlers Corner would be location to look for them.

Joe had the camp set up in no time. It did not take long to start the fire and get food prepared. It could be a cold night in the mountains. Earl was busy trying to set up radio communications, someone had to be out there to talk to.

Being under the big evergreen tree would keep a lot of snow off the tent and mean less preparation when the storm broke. They probably would not have much snow on the tent, but as soon as they departed the cover of the tree, there would be plenty.

Suddenly, there was a crackling on the radio. Earl jumped to his feet and grabbed the radio and listened closely. "This Is Snow One, repeat, this is Snow One, can anyone read this transmission?" Waiting a minute, Earl again repeated the call on the radio.

"Snow One, Snow One, this is Primrose One, do you read?" came the call.

"Primrose One, This is Snow One, Read you clearly but with interference."

"Snow One, what is your current location?"

"Primrose One, we are currently at Rustlers Corner, camp set up and waiting to hear from just about anyone now. Do you have new information for us, Primrose One?" Earl asked.

"Snow One, we have established contact with your camp Zulu Two. Unable to contact Camp Zulu itself. Zulu Two apparently has a land line to communicate with your base. They have advised that you stay put tonight and see what the weather looks like in the morning. Arctic Cat will not be able to make the mountain passes tonight. Very heavy snow below your location. If needed they will attempt to get something up to you. How are you fixed with supplies and equipment?"

"Primrose One, we have plenty of supplies. Have enough equipment and material to spend the night. Longer if necessary. What is the weather situation in the area?" Earl asked.

"Snow One, the weather does not look good for the next twelve hours. There is a major storm that developed several hours ago and does not look like it will break for a while. Our location seems to be above the major snow line. We have a fix on your location so we will be able to communicate regularly as necessary," Primrose One stated.

"Primrose One, do you have a visual on the fire that is burning on the east side of Echo?" Earl inquired.

"Snow One, that is a negative at this time, we are just around the side of Enchanted and not able to see the East side. If we get a chance we will go around Enchanted and take a look, in fact, we will send one of our machines around and take a look, and get back to you. It will take about thirty minutes to complete the trip, will get back to you. Primrose out."

Well, thought Earl, we might just as well get ready for a long night. It should be about 25 degrees and about twelve inches of snow by morning. Settling down for a quick bite to eat, the two discussed how they were going to handle the night watch for the fire. Probably nothing to worry about, but it needed to be considered.

The pine forest would slow the storm down at the ground level. That is why they wanted to get to the Rustlers Corner for the night.

"Joe," Earl spoke, "Do you think we will need to set up the snowmobile for heat tonight if it only gets to around 25 degrees? What about the possibility of throwing up the snow fence on the side, that would keep some snow off the tent?"

Joe thought about it for a moment, "Good idea about the snow fence, I had not gotten to that yet, but should put it up. I don't think we will need the snowmobile heater for the night. We will determine that as the night goes on."

Time was passing slowly for the two, only two thirty in the afternoon. Seemed like eight thirty. After a few more minutes, the radio again broke the silence. "Snow One, Snow One, this is Primrose One, do you copy?"

Earl grabbed the radio and replied. "Primrose One, this is Snow One, I copy."

"Snow One, the disturbance on the side of Echo seems to be under control due to the snow, there is no report of fire and the snow is light on that side of the mountain. Maybe it got snowed under. Will keep an eye on it for the next several hours. Report from your Zulu Two says that Zulu One will attempt to get the Arctic Cat up the mountain at daybreak. If you need something or some emergency comes up, please contact us and we will get word back to Zulu Two for you. Zulu Two is only a mile from our camp, we will try and get one of our machines over to them if necessary. Primrose One out."

"Primrose One, thanks for your help, you make the night easier to take knowing you are up there watching over us" Earl commented.

"Snow One, we were in your position only a few weeks ago, we know what you are experiencing. Settle down for the night, play cards and enjoy the beautiful nature of the mountain if you can."

"Earl" Joe asked, "Why do you suppose that we are the only ones stuck up here on the mountain, we seem to be the only one in real deep snow for the night?"

Earl looked at Joe as if to say, 'well it might be a good thing we were able to spend the night here in this place instead of further up the mountain.' Nothing needed to be said about the lodging facilities up in the poplar stand where there would be no cover at all.

It was starting to get dark by four thirty because of the heavy snow. There was very little wind. The old pine tree just stood tall as if to be honored to have guest for the night. There was very little movement in the area. Several small birds and grouse in the area. Deer must have sensed that it would be wise to move out prior to the storm. They sure did not leave any messages for the two to follow.

Earl took the time to build a small fire out of some small twigs and low branches that were dry enough to burn. "Something about having a small fire the old pine and fresh snow that makes a man want to sing," Earl muttered.

Joe looked at him and gave a small gesture of welcome to some entertainment. "Are you going to sing originals tonight or someone else's proven songs?" Joe asked. "I know you have plenty of camp fireside songs that can entertain us for several hours."

After several hours of singing and storytelling, Earl decided to try and raise Primrose One again and tell them that they were going to sign off for the night. There appeared to be nothing more for them to do. "Primrose One, this is Snow One, do you copy?"

"Snow One, this is Primrose One, we do copy, what can we do for you?"

"Primrose One, we are going to turn in for the night, everything seems to be under control now that we know you are watching over us. If you still have contact with Zulu Two, please relay the word to them we are good for the night, thank you for being there Primrose," Earl laid the radio down and stretched out in his sleeping bag.

"Not how I planned to spend the night, Joe" Earl quipped. "I planned to be out in the village enjoying the harvest party and watching the kids have the time of their life. I hope that Zulu contacted the families and told them we were going to do a little late season camping on the mountain."

As the night drew later and later, there was very little noise in the pine forest. Only the whippoorwill calling in the night. An occasional pine cone falling from the old tree. A very uneventful night.

About five thirty in the morning, Joe opened his tent to check the weather. The old pine tree limbs that had protected them for the night were heavy with snow. But little in the immediate area of the tent and snowmobile. It apparently did not get as cold as anticipated. Joe was very comfortable as he crawled out of his bag.

Being quiet not to wake Earl, Joe stepped out of the tent to put on his clothes and shoes. He could sit on the snowmobile and watch the beginning of a new day. The storm apparently had finally passed on. Time to get out and check the new snow depth. Pushing the low limbs aside, he stepped out from the protection of the big pine. He was astonished to see the amount of snow that had fallen since they parked in the area the night before.

At six, Joe called Earl to get him started. They needed to be ready to move when the word came in, if it did come in.

"Earl, do you want eggs and bacon for breakfast or just cold cereal?" Joe asked.

"Cold cereal will be fine with me, do you have the coffee ready?" Earl asked.

"You bet" Joe came back. "It has been ready for fifteen minutes. I wanted to make sure it was strong enough for you before you got up" Joe said jokingly.

"Any word on the radio this morning Joe?" Earl asked.

"Nothing yet, but is a bit early for someone who may be enjoying a vacation and not needing to be up at this hour" Joe came back. "Earl, do you think we should try base again before calling Primrose?" Joe queried.

After having breakfast, the two started to check the real depth of the snow outside from under the protecting pine tree. A couple cups of coffee and a quick check of the weather, everything seemed to be looking good. Breaking camp, Joe wondered if they should continue up the hill or wait for confirmation from base camp.

"Well," Earl yelled out, "It must be time to see if we can get anyone on the radio now. After all it is almost seven in the morning."

As he reached for the radio, it suddenly came to life itself "Snow One, Snow One, this is Camp Zulu, do you copy? Snow One, do you copy this message?"

Earl took the radio and calmly answered, "Camp Zulu, you bet we copy, where have you folks been. We have already had breakfast and were about ready to break camp. What do we do now?"

"Snow One do you think you can proceed up the mountain with the supplies? Zulu Two still needs those supplies you are carrying, that is if you haven't consumed them overnight. How much snow is at your location? Do we need to send up the Arctic Cat? By the way, Zulu Two only received two inches of new snow, they were wondering what was keeping you."

"Zulu, We will be able to spend the day here, there is about thirty inches of new snow, the trail up ahead is subject to snow slides and dangerous for us to be out there. We are waiting for you to tell us which way to proceed." Earl informed Zulu base.

"Snow One, Stay in place, we will send the Arctic cat up with the mobile room, that will give you a place to leave equipment and go with the Arctic Cat to Zulu Twos location, do you copy?"

"Zulu base," Earl came back, "we do not need the mobile, as we are under this great big friendly pine that has taken care of us for the night, she will watch our equipment. You just send us the cat and we will be out of here."

"Snow One, the Arctic Cat is on the way, standby and have the coffee ready, they should be there in less than an hour."

"Roger, will have the coffee ready and waiting for the cat." Earl commented.

"Primrose One, are you still up there?" Earl continued his radio dialog.

"That's affirmative, Snow One, We are still here, good to hear that you have radio contact with your base, We have talked to your Zulu Two, they are ready for you to continue up the trail."

"Primrose if you have time, why don't you meet us for lunch at Zulu Twos location, we will have a chance to go over the events of the night." Earl asked.

"Sorry, Snow One, We have another place to be tonight. We would like to take you up on your offer, but duty calls us elsewhere."

As the day drew on, the Arctic cat arrived on schedule and Joe and Earl went on up the hill, leaving the snowmobile under the big pine tree along with some other small equipment. As they left Zulu Two that afternoon, Earl asked if they heard from Primrose One since early morning.

Nothing at all, they seemed to have slipped away into the blue sky, Nobody knows where they were from or where they were headed, they were not registered for an overnight on that location.

The trip back to the big pine standing at Rustlers Comer was uneventful. Recovering the equipment and moving down the mountain, Joe wondered about the fire, Rival two and about where Primrose One was and where they might have gotten off to.

EUROPE

Sitting at the desk, Joe received what appeared to be an unusual request. "Joe," stated the voice on the intercom, "do you know any European languages."

Joe, momentarily startled by the request, finally answered, "Yes, I speak and read German and French."

"Good," came a reply, "have you many clothes to pack for a trip?" "Do you know anyone who would like to accompany you?" "We have an immediate need to send three people to Europe for about 75 days, can you handle it?"

Joe was quick to come back this time, "You bet I can handle it. Will Earl be going with me?" Who might be the third person? What about Michelle, She speaks, reads and writes several languages also?"

"Joe, lets hold off on the other people for now, we need to find out what all is involved in getting there. I don't suppose that you have a current passport? If so, will it be good for about 6 months?" the voice continued.

Joe did not recognize the voice on the intercom. Who would be inviting him to make such a great trip. He had been looking at his finances to see if he could even afford such a trip just this past week.

"Joe, we will be back with you in a day or so about the possibilities of you and two others going to Germany, France and Spain. We need to look at the total package and cost factors for three for that period of time. But you are seriously interested in going?" the voice asked.

"Yes I am" Joe replied.

As Joe set in his chair for the next few minutes with his mind wandering in French, he was abruptly brought back to awareness when Earl came in for a short conference.

"Earl did you get a call about going to Europe for several months?" Joe asked. "I just got a request for my level of interest in going and two other people to go also. Did you get a call?"

"No," Earl said, "I have just come from the laboratory and not close to any phones."

"I asked if you and Michelle would be able to go or be considered as the other two. But the voice, which I did not recognize, simply said that I was to be patient," Joe reflected. "We could have a lot of fun in Europe for several months. I haven't been there since I was stationed there nearly twenty years ago."

"Joe, do you think they will let Michelle go along? They have not let her travel with us in the past." Earl Asked. "It would be nice if she could go on this trip, she needs to get on one of these trips to get a better education of what it is we do in the field. She certainly deserves the opportunity to go. She speaks several languages"

As they were discussing this turn of events, Michelle appeared at the door, with a great big smile on her face. "Joe, what did you tell Mr. Millo. He just got off the intercom with me and said that you wanted me to go to Europe with you and Earl. What a great thing to say. I would really like to go on this trip. What about you Earl, are you excited?"

"I haven't been asked yet. I have been out of the office and not available to talk to anyone about it. I just found out that Joe has asked and that he indicated you should be on this trip. I fully concur with Joe on that point. But I have not been asked. Is it for sure that you are going, or is he just checking out your level of interest.?" Earl stated.

"Just checking on my level of interest and the fact that Joe recommended me," Michelle answered. "I am really excited about even being considered," she continued "You two have so much experience on this type research, it will be great working with you guys."

"Joe," the intercom broke in again, "I cannot get a hold of Earl to ask him if he would be interested, but I suppose by now you have already called him. I just finished a few minutes ago with Michelle, You don't know how you must have brightened her day. She is very excited, I bet she has gone home and started to pack even though I suggested that she wait for final confirmation."

"No sir, she is in my office and is really a very happy young lady. Earl come in only a few minutes after you called me, we have discussed it very briefly" Joe commented.

"We are currently trying to get Michelle back to earth. Just what did you tell her to get her so excited? I have never seen her at such a high." Earl spoke.

"Well, If the three of you can get passports and packed with in ten days, we will send all of you over for about 75 days. It will be in France, Germany and Spain, maybe a short research project in England. Do all of you think you can handle it?" The voice inquired. "I suppose I should ask Earl if he would be interested, after all, he may want to stay home and finish the paper work."

"That's all right sir, I will be sure to get most of my packing done tonight, just in case you move up the departure date." Earl said with great excitement.

"I will talk to the three of you in the morning to discuss the details and how you are to enjoy yourselves while there. We have a very special package I think all of you will really enjoy," said the voice on the intercom. "What do you say if we get together at 9:30 in the coffee shop on first floor of your building."

The three were so excited that they forgot to check for any further information.

"Michelle, do you have a valid passport? I know Joe and I both have?" Earl asked Michelle.

"My family was going to take me on a trip to the orient last fall, I was ready to go when I got this job offer, now I will really have a chance to use my passport. Wow, Am I excited. Thanks Joe for suggesting my name. I will be forever indebted to you for this opportunity." Michelle could hardly contain her excitement.

"What do you think your folks will say when they find out, Michelle," Joe asked. "Do you think they will have any reservations about you going with us?"

"I don't really care, I have looked forward to getting out in the field anywhere, just anywhere. And now to get to go with the two best in the field, what an opportunity. Besides, my folks are still in the orient. They are not due back for another month or so" Michelle answered as she was beginning to loose her voice with all the excitement.

"Well, we had better return to our work places, we have to get the reports finished and insure that all is clear here or we won't be going anywhere," Earl stated. "We still have several day's work to get caught up on. We do want to be ready for this trip."

At the meeting the next day, They were fully briefed on what was expected of them while doing research. Then, Mr. Millo gave them the best news any researcher in Europe could hope for.

"The research offices in Europe will only be available for four days a week. So to insure that you folks have enough to do to keep busy, the company is providing each of you with a long term EURAIL pass and two nights hotel accommodations in various cities of your choice while there. You do not have to be traveling every weekend, only when you want. All we ask is that you keep records for future bookkeeping."

The next few days were filled with excitement in the offices occupied by the three. Other staff members came by to see if they were sick and not able to go. Most other staff members were very supportive and helpful of how to enjoy Europe.

On the day of departure, Mr. Millo and several program managers were at the airport to see them off. Each one had something smart to say and showed signs of envy. Finally, one of them spoke seriously, "If you ever do such a good job and get yourselves promoted into management jobs, guess where you will be on days like today?"

Joe was first into the line for loading on the plane, Michelle second followed by Earl. Michelle spoke softly, "I do believe that some of them wanted to be in our places. I thought I detected a bit of real envy."

"Mr. Millo, used to go on an these overseas assignments. But not since he moved into management. There is not enough for management to do on a trip like this. After all, four days a week, a free train pass for every weekend and hotels paid for, what a deal. I know we are going to enjoy this trip." Earl informed the other two.

Their first stop was to be in Frankfurt, Germany. As the big plane stopped at the terminal, they waited patiently for the big crowd to get off the plane, Joe knew that there would be a big crowd standing at the immigrations desk and therefore he was in no hurry, besides, they did not have to be to work for two days.

As the line thinned out on the plane, they moved out and into the immigration area, looking for the gates that stated Non-EC countries people. That line moved quickly as most of the people on the flight were from Europe and could process through the EC line.

Their next encounter would be with the folks at the baggage claim area. "Hope everything made it all right," Michelle commented. She had never taken a trip like this before, so she was understandably a bit nervous.

"Baggage will take a few minutes to come down," Joe stated. "It takes a while for them to off load the plane and get it all on the belts. We can relax for a moment."

In about ten minutes, luggage started to appear on the conveyor belt.

"I did not realize that two hundred people could have so much luggage," Michelle stated emphatically.

Clearing customs and out the control doors and into the open foyer, they look for information. Someone had told them that the primary information desk was on the upper level near Delta airlines on the B concourse. They decide that they could get information from the downtown information desk also.

Going down the escalator towards the Flughafen Bahnhof(train station) they see the sign that says there is McDonald's located OA. "Where would that be?" Earl asked.

"Somewhere on the lower level of the A Concourse," Joe answered. "The "0" is the lower lever in Europe. The "A" is A Concourse."

"Let's get a burger before we go downtown," Michelle suggested.

"Good idea." Earl responded.

"We can either get something here or wait until we get to the downtown station, they have one in there also, it will be larger and therefore quicker for service," Joe informed them.

"All right, how long is it to downtown by train?" Earl asked.

"Should be about 10 minutes by train. It doesn't take long and the train stops at the main station. Let's wait and get a better choice. "Joe directs them.

As they head towards the trains, located underground on B Concourse, they see the small schedule board telling them the next train is leaving in ten minutes, from Gleiss 1A. Joe informs them "Gleiss is the German word for gate or track."

Getting the tickets from the small vending machines they set and wait for the train.

"I think I can like this type of assignment," Joe commented.

As the S-14 train pulls into the Flughafen Bahnhof, they get on and have a seat. People are certainly friendly and the ride is short.

The S-14 takes only about 12 minutes to arrive at the Frankfurt-Main Hauptbahnhof. Getting off and going up both sets of escalators to the surface, they see McDonalds and Tourist Information both across from Gleiss 24. Also, there is a small Gepack im Schliessfach (selfstorage lockers) in the area.

"Joe and Michelle, let's put the luggage away first and then get a bite to eat" Earl suggested. "We don't need to be carrying this stuff around until we find the hotel."

"Earl, I have a suggestion," Michelle said with a smile on her face, "Why don't you put the luggage away. Joe and I will go for the food."

"No way." Earl said. "It should be the other way around, remember who is in charge of this operation, as far as it goes."

"I do think each should take care of their own," Joe finally answered. "We are all big people and have our own responsibilities. Who has all the DM for the lockers. Should only take three DM per locker. We do have enough to fill one each."

Soon they were all looking at the variety of places to get a bite to eat. A wide variety of German and other local foods, also several other country foods. Outside and across the street they see a Burger King and Pizza Hut.

"Sure is no shortage of American influence in the food business here in this area," Michelle noticed and commented. "I hear that there are a lot of German restaurants or what they call Guest Haus or something like that. But I also heard that they are not open early in the day, where do people eat, burger places, I guess."

Checking the many places they decide to go local instead of burger. Not a bad choice. After getting something to eat, they head for the information center. The friendly lady working behind the counter is very helpful. She sets them up with a nice European three star hotel only a block off the bus stop.

She shows them how to read the bus maps and the ticket machines. She wishes them farewell and they are off to get their luggage. They can get it all on the bus and to the hotel in a couple minutes.

Reading the bus schedule and catching the bus was a bit challenging for them, but they were able to catch the second bus. Riding the bus for only a couple minutes, they arrive at the hotel stop. Taking their baggage up to the hotel and checking in, they get rooms on the same floor but at opposite ends of the hall.

Earl and Joe were given a suite while Michelle had a basic room. Her room had the basic necessities, bathroom facilities but not much more. But then what does she need. She plans only to be there for night time, and gone during the day and weekends. This was going to work out fine for all of them.

Michelle was content just to rest for a while, she wanted to freshen up and take a breather. Just to get a chance to relax. Earl and Joe were eager to hit the new environment.

Neither had been in Frankfurt before, so they were eager to get started. But being the two gentlemen they were, they consent to giving Michelle an hour to get her self ready or they would go without her.

"You guys ought to consider giving me a little more time than that," Michelle requested.

Michelle complied with their request. After an hour, she returned to their room and knocked on their door.

"You guys ready to go now that I am here?"

For a moment there was no answer. Finally Earl came to the door and said they would be ready in a minute and for her to come in.

Searching all over the town they spend hours just riding the trains, strassenbahns and local busses. It was a great time for them.

They located the route to the research building located on the Romer Platz.

"What a beautiful location for an office," Joe Commented. "This place was founded by the Romans many centuries ago, what a piece of history."

As the work week started for the three, they were more than impressed with all they could do, movies, arts, theater and general sightseeing. Waiting for their first weekend to come up they were eagerly discussing how they could see so much in such a short time.

"Earl how are you going to divide up your free time, where are you going? Do you mind if I come along with you sometime? You do realize that I have never been outside of the states and haven't got a clue on how to get around, but am very willing to learn if you teach and show me," Michelle began to ask.

Earl came back quickly, "Michelle, we are here as a team, you are certainly part of it, Thanks to Joe for recommending you. You are going to be traveling with us most of the time. We are really going to see it all, Berlin, Dachau, Bertchesgarten, Austria, Switzerland, and you are going with us. That is unless you find something else to do for a weekend."

"What more could I ask for, Two big brothers and a free train ticket every weekend. You guys are just going to spoil me. I am very thankful that you guys took a chance on bringing me over here. It could have been a three man team just as easy. But you ask for me, is there a specific reason for asking for me?" Michelle said with a lot of excitement.

"Michelle, you deserve just as much a chance to come over as anyone else. Besides, you have very high standards for the company, and yourself. I don't know of anyone else to come here with other than Earl. Him and I have been together so long now, we know how each other thinks" Joe said to Michelle.

"You need a chance to get out and prove yourself so they will send you more often." Earl also responded to her question.

Spending weekends on the train, the three went in every direction, East, North and South. They knew they were going West on assignment soon. that meant they would be able to see France, Luxembourg, Belgium and Holland a little later. They were amazed at the different life styles involved in just Germany alone. There seemed to be a different culture in every state in Germany.

Dialect was certainly very noticeable. Traveling in Northern Germany, they spent several weekends in Hamlin, Hanover, Schlesvig and Bremen. Then off to the East, Berlin, Poland and the old Czech Republic and Slovakia.

Turning their weekends South, they went to Wien, Austria and deep into the mountains of Switzerland. They traveled so much they almost knew the train staff by first name.

One weekend was devoted to getting into Italy. The overnight train was a real peaceful experience. None of them had ever traveled by train overnight before.

"This certainly is the way to go in the future," Michelle insisted. "We travel during the night as we have seen most of the countryside between Frankfurt and the Italian border. This gives us time to see the country side during the early morning hours. I am really happy to be on this Italian express."

It didn't take long and their assignment to Frankfurt was nearing an end.

"Better call Mr. Millo and get started on our next assignment." Earl slowly commented one day.

"Yes, all good things must come to an end," Joe replied. "But there aren't to many jobs around like this one where we work four days and get three paid vacation days."

"I am really looking forward to seeing France as much as we have covered this end of Europe" Michelle said excitedly. "We are really going to be knowledgeable of most of Europe by the time we finish this assignment. Do they get these types of assignments often Earl?" she asked.

"No, I have been with them for twelve years and have never seen one like this. We may get to visit another research center for a day or two, but never this long or especially these types of benefits. They must have thought that there would be trouble filling positions for this research by the way they threw on the extras for us." Earl replied.

"I would have been willing to come even without the benefits, what about you Joe?" Michelle asked.

"Yes, I would have been first in line anyway" Joe answered with a bit of excitement.

The following Monday, Earl called Mr. Millo to get further instructions on the next part of the trip.

Their follow on assignment took them first to Madrid, Spain and then into Barcelona. From there they were to take a train up to Paris for three weeks.

"Lyon to Paris via the TGV" Michelle spoke out. "I have been wanting to take the TGV for years, and now I get my chance. I wished we were on a TGV coming up from Barcelona."

Earl looked at her and decided to throw her a slow curve, "Michelle, our tickets do not cover the cost of the TGV. We are not able to ride them. We are mandated to the slow inter regional and express trains."

"You got to be kidding me," Michelle exploded. "You are telling me we were able to use any of the trains in Germany including the ICE trains but we cannot use the TGV in France?"

"Just kidding, Michelle, hold on to your hat. We are going to Lyon this weekend. We are going to cover most of France as best we can in the three weekends we have available. Maybe we can talk Mr. Millo into an extra weekend." Earl cut her off as he could detect her boiling point coming up fast. "You should know we have unlimited train travel in any country we travel in. That means here in France also."

Upon arriving in Paris, they realized they were to relearn the Metro system all over again.

Paris Metro runs like other systems, only a bit more sporty to follow. They had to learn a bit more about Paris.

Major points along the routes, as the Metro runs in many directions. Learning the new system, they quickly started to explore Paris. They only have three weekends to spend in France, that meant they were really going to have to plan their travels.

Their three weeks in France was gone before they knew it.

It was time to move on up to London and Glasgow. They knew they would enjoy those two spots, they have been forewarned about having a good time in those two cities.

"How are we going to get to England?" Joe asked Earl. We have the slow overnight ferry, which also runs daily. There is the SeaCat, the new one, really supposed to be the best way to cross now. There is the HoverCraft and the Jetfoil. Both are really good methods."

"What would you like to take, Michelle?" Earl asked giving her a chance for input in the decision.

"I think I would like to take the fastest way, I don't like water and I want to get into England quickly." Michelle responded. "I think I would like to try either the SeaCat or Jetfoil. I hear that you don't see much on the Hovercraft. There is no way I want to be going on a four or five hour ferry ride just to get to England. I have more important things to get on with."

"Joe are you in favor of the SeaCat? That Catamaran is supposed to be a real beautiful experience. I think that will be the way we travel, Michelle has already voted and I am inclined to agree with her." Earl questioned.

Several days later the three were on the SeaCat headed for the Dover Port in England. The big catamaran gliding smoothly across the channel waters. Plenty of other ship traffic on the English Channel. But they were standing up front watching all the action.

Soon the White Cliffs of Dover showed up on the horizon. What an impressive sight, a great big white mountain, a sea port and small town in one place. Their ride was over in almost no time.

Taking the available train to London, they checked into the Victoria Station information center upon arrival.

This time it was Michelle's turn to make room reservations, as they had been practicing and taking turns in duties and responsibilities in each city they visited.

"Let's get our rooms near Trafalger Square," Joe requested.

"Good idea," Michelle replied. "I will get us something and be right back, in the meantime, you guys go over to Burger King or up to McDonald's and have a cup of coffee. I will find us something."

With that vote of self confidence, Joe and Earl went out of the area, leaving Michelle to find a place by herself. They knew she could use the system by now, after all, they had been showing her in every city how to work hotel rooms.

After two weeks in London, They had a week in Glasgow. Boarding the InterCity Express 225 train from London Victoria station, they were in Glasgow in about seven hours. Finding a room quickly as it was midafternoon and places would soon start filling up with hikers and real tourist.

"We are getting a short end here in Scotland, we don't have a full weekend to travel out of town." Earl comments.

"We really need to talk to Mr. Millo and see if we can't leave on Tuesday of next week from here in Glasgow," Michelle insisted. "After all, there is a lot of Scotland we will not be able to visit during the week, much less on one weekend. We really need two weekends here. They tell me that the Inverness area is beautiful along with the train ride up to the northern tip in the Thurso area."

"Michelle, we should not press our luck, we have had several months here with the company really putting out a great deal for us. We probably better be ready to return on Saturday as planned," Earl stated rather strongly.

"I will be talking to him this afternoon, will relay your preferences on the return date, but don't hold your breath Michelle." Earl informed both Michelle and Joe.

The research work for the day was finished ahead of schedule and they had an hour to spare.

"Can't call Mr. Millo until 4:30 this afternoon, let's take a local bus and ride it out of town for a bit," Joe injected in the afternoon decision making process.

The three were back in Glasgow by 7:00 PM and waiting for time to call Mr. Millo.

"You two go down and order our dinner meal, I will be there before long," Earl insisted.

As they left the hotel room, Earl went to the phone and called Mr. Millo.

"Mr. Millo, we have a little problem on this end. Michelle and both of us want a weekend to go up into northern Scotland, but you have us scheduled to return on Saturday of this week. I don't suppose you can change any airline tickets this late in the process, can you, Mr. Millo?" Earl said begging.

"Earl, I needed to talk to you about that, I need for you folks to go up to Inverness and over to Edinburgh for one day each. You will get your extra weekend and I get what I need at the sometime" Mr. Millo stated.

"Your new departure date will be Wednesday at 0950 from Edinburgh back home. I hope that doesn't make anyone so sad. We both get what we need or want should I say," Mr. Millo informed Earl.

"You have my vote, Mr. Millo," Earl stated emphatically, "I am also sure that Michelle and Joe will concur. I shall be glad to inform them of the new departure time."

As Earl entered the dining room, both Joe and Michelle were looking straight at him. "Better make this good," he thought to himself.

"Well folks, it is like this. Mr. Millo was really understanding of our desires to spend another weekend here in Scotland. He checked his big book and concurred with it under one condition, we must spend a day in Inverness and one in Edinburgh with a flight out of there on Wednesday." Earl told them both.

"Yes!," Michelle almost yelled out. "I knew you could talk him into another weekend. I really like this assignment, It has certainly been a very rewarding one for me. I know also that this is one of those once in a life time deals. Well, I have really enjoyed it. Thanks for bringing me along guys. I really mean that," she stated with small tears of excitement starting to flow.

The following weekend was spent on the Western and Northern tip of Scotland and back to Inverness for the day there. Getting to Edinburgh early on Tuesday, they were going directly to work.

They checked their luggage into the short term storage lockers and were going to pick it up in the afternoon. The people at the center were expecting them early and they didn't want to be late.

They could have left Inverness the night before, but there was a tour going out to the Loch Ness area, all three wanted to go, so they compromised and decided to get up early in the morning.

As they arrived at the research center, they were told to wait in the lounge for a minute until credentials were checked. They thought that was strange, no one had asked for credentials anywhere else.

After a minute waiting, they were greeted by the head of the research center in Edinburgh. "Folks, I have some very important news to pass on to you, from all the reports I have been getting from your people, we are now going to release you to the city of

Edinburgh and provide you with an all day tour of the city and area. There is only one hitch, You must be willing to take along one individual who insist on going along. I know a lot of people who would be grateful to be in your place today. You are in for a real treat. The company has seen fit to send over one top level executive to see to it that you folks enjoy the day. Mr. Millo will you come out and Join your working staff."

"Certainly, will be glad to join them. I have been waiting for this day for almost three months. I know how excited these three people are. They have done a lot of research and traveled a lot according to the bills we have been receiving." Mr. Millo quipped.

As the day drew to an end, they were treated to a full party and a five star hotel for the night.

Mr. Millo, and other company executives met them in the morning and departed for the airport.

After they return to their respective offices, they are called upon frequently to interpret data from their reports. There will be plenty of time to reflect on what they had seen.

Thanking Mr. Millo almost every day, Michelle was always reminding him how happy she was to be able to be part of the research trip.